This book belongs to

....

Usborne
Illustrated
Classics for
Children

Contents

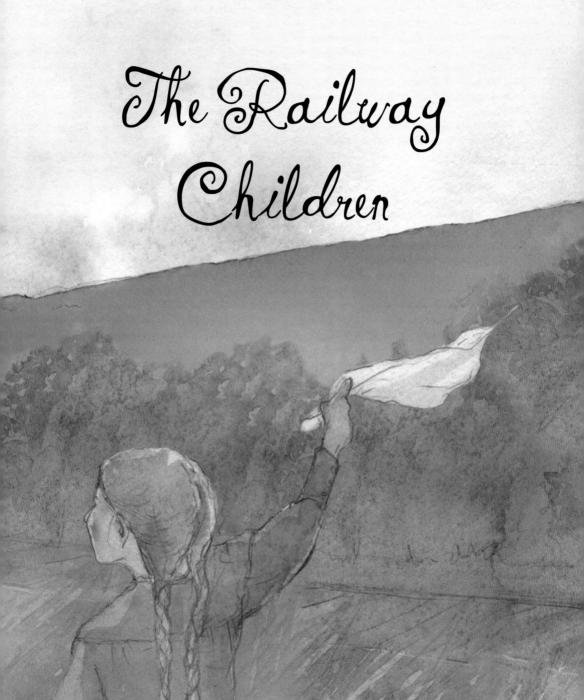

The Railway Children

E. Nesbit (1858-1924)

Edith Nesbit wrote a hundred years ago, when most people rode by horse, not car, and television hadn't been invented. Her stories are full of excitement, adventure and magic. *The Railway Children*, first published in 1906, is one of her most famous books. It has been adapted for television four times and has twice been made into a film.

Chapter 1
Change

It all began at Peter's birthday party. The servants were just bringing out the birthday cake, when the doorbell clanged sharply.

"Oh dear!" exclaimed Father. "Who can that be? Start without me, everyone. I'll be back in a minute."

Peering into the hallway, Peter saw Father leading two men into his study.

"Who are they, Mother?" asked his sister, Phyllis.

"I don't know," said
Mother, frowning.
"Stay here. I'm going
to find out."

Mother disappeared into the study for ages.
"What's going on?" asked Phyllis.
"We'll just have to wait and see," replied
Bobbie, the eldest.

Mother emerged just as the front door slammed shut. Bobbie saw a carriage and horses driving rapidly away into the night. Mother's face was icy white and her eyes glittered with tears.

"Where's Father?" demanded Peter, running into the empty study.

"He's gone away." Mother was shaking now. Bobbie reached for her hand and held it tight.

"But he hasn't even packed his clothes," said Phyllis.

"He had to go quickly – on business," Mother replied.

"Was it to do with the Government?" asked Peter. Father worked in a Government office.

"Yes. Don't ask me questions, darlings. I can't tell you anything. Please just go to bed."

Upstairs, the children tried endlessly to work out where Father had gone. The next few days were just as strange.

All the maids left. Then a FOR SALE sign went up outside the house. The beautiful furniture was sold and meals now consisted of plain, cheap food. Mother was hardly ever at home.

15

"What's happening?" asked Peter, finally. "Please tell us."

"We've got to play at being poor for a bit," Mother replied. "We're going to leave London, and live far away in the countryside."

"Father is going to be away for some time," she went on. "But everything will come right in the end, I promise."

Chapter 2
A coal thief

After a long, long journey, they arrived at the new house, late at night.

Mother rushed around, digging sheets out of suitcases.

The next day, Bobbie, Peter and Phyllis woke early to explore. They raced outside until they came to a red-brick bridge.

Suddenly there was a shriek and a snort and a train shot out from under it.

"It's exactly like a dragon," Peter shouted above the noise. "Did you feel the hot air from its breath?"

"Perhaps it's going to London," Phyllis yelled.

"Father might still be there," shrieked Bobbie. "If it's a magic dragon, it'll send our love to Father. Let's wave."

They pulled out their handkerchiefs and waved them in the breeze. Out of a first class carriage window a hand waved back. It was an old gentleman's hand, holding a newspaper.

After that, the children waved every day, rain or shine, at the old gentleman on the 9:15 train to London.

The weather grew colder. Mother sat in her icy bedroom wrapped in shawls, writing stories to earn money for them all.

Bobbie, Peter and Phyllis didn't notice the cold much. They were too busy playing. But one morning, it snowed so much they had to stay inside.

"Please let me light a fire, Mother," begged Bobbie. "We're all freezing."

"Not until tonight, I'm afraid. We can't afford to burn coal all day. Put on more clothes if you're chilly."

Peter was furious. "I'm the man in this family now," he stormed. "And I think we ought to be warm."

Over the next few days Peter began to disappear without saying where he was going.

"I can't understand it," Mother said soon after. "The coal never seems to run out."

"Let's follow Pete," Bobbie whispered to Phyllis. "I'm sure he's up to something."

They trailed him all the way to the station, and watched him pile a cart with coal from a huge heap.

Then suddenly, Peter screamed.

A hand had shot out of the
darkness and grabbed
him by the shoulder.

It was Mr. Perks, the station master. "Don't you know stealing is wrong?" he shouted.

"Wasn't stealing. I was mining for treasure," sulked Peter.

"That treasure belongs to the railway, young man, not you."

"He shouldn't have done it, Mr. Perks," said Bobbie, shocked. "But he was only trying to help Mother. He's really sorry, aren't you, Pete?" She gave him a kick and Peter muttered an apology.

"Accepted," said Perks. "But don't do it again."

"I hate being poor," grumbled Peter, kicking the cobbles on their way home. "And Mother deserves better than this."

Soon after, Mother got very sick. Bobbie didn't know how they were going to pay for her medicines, until she had a brilliant idea.

She wrote a letter to the old gentleman on the 9:15 train to London and asked Mr. Perks to give it to him.

Dear Mr. (we don't know your name),

Mother is sick and we can't afford the things the doctor says she needs. This is the list:

Medicine   Port Wine

Fruit   Soda water

I don't know who else to ask.

Father will pay you back when he comes home, or I will when I grow up.

Bobbie

P.S. Please give them to Mr. Perks, the station master, and Pete will fetch them.

The very next day, a huge hamper appeared, filled with medicines, as well as red roses, chocolates and lavender perfume. A week later, Bobbie, Peter and Phyllis made a banner and waved it at the 9:15 train. It said:

But Mother was furious when she found out. "You must never ask strangers for things," she raged.

Bobbie was nearly in tears. "I didn't mean to be naughty."

"I know, my darling," said Mother. "But you mustn't tell everyone we're poor. We have enough to live on – just. Now we won't say any more about it."

Chapter 3
Red for danger

They all felt miserable for upsetting
Mother. "I know what will cheer us up!"
said Bobbie. "We can ask Mr. Perks for the
magazines people leave on trains. They'd be
fun to read."

"Let's climb down the cliff and walk along the track to the station," suggested Peter. "We've never gone that way before."

"I don't want to. It doesn't look safe." Phyllis sounded frightened.

"Baby! Scaredy-cat!" teased Peter.

"It's all right, Phil," Bobbie comforted her. "The cliff isn't that steep."

"Two against one," crowed Peter. "Come on, Phil, you'll enjoy it."

Slowly Phyllis followed her brother and sister, muttering, "I still don't want to..."

34

They scrambled down the cliff. Phyllis tumbled down the last bit where the steps had crumbled away, and tore her dress.

Now her red petticoat flapped through the tear as she walked.

"There!" she announced. "I told you this would be horrible, and it is!"

"No, it isn't," disagreed Peter.

"What's that noise?" asked Bobbie suddenly.
A strange sound, like far off thunder, began
and stopped. Then it started again, getting
louder and more rumbling.

"Look at that tree!" cried Peter. The tree was moving, not like a normal tree when the wind blows, but all in one piece.

All the trees on the bank seemed to be slowly sliding downhill, like a marching army.

Suddenly, rocks, trees, grasses, bushes and earth gathered speed in a deafening roar and collapsed in a heap on the railway track.

"I don't like it!" shrieked Phyllis. "It's much too magic for me!"

"It's all coming down," said Peter in a shaky voice. Then he cried out, "Oh!"

The others looked at him. "The 11:29 train! It'll be along any minute. There'll be a terrible accident."

"Can we run to the station and tell them?" Bobbie began.

"No time. We need to warn the driver somehow. What can we do?"

"Our red petticoats!" Bobbie exclaimed. "Red for danger! We'll tear them up and use them as flags."

"We can't rip our clothes!" Phyllis objected. "What will Mother say?"

"She won't mind." Bobbie was undoing her petticoat as she spoke. "Don't you see, Phil, if we don't stop the train in time, people might be killed?"

They quickly snapped thin branches off the
nearby trees, tore up the petticoats and made
them into flags.

"Two each. Wave one in each hand, and stand
on the track so the train can see us," Peter
directed. "Then jump out of the way."

Phyllis was gasping with fright. "It's dangerous! I don't like it!"

"Think of saving the train," Bobbie implored. "That's what matters most!"

"It's coming," called Peter, though his voice was instantly wiped out in a whirlwind of sound.

As the roaring train thundered nearer and nearer, Bobbie waved her flags furiously. She was sure it was no good, that the train would never see them in time...

"MOVE!" shouted Peter, as the train's steam surrounded them in a cloud of white. But Bobbie couldn't. She had to make it stop.

With a judder and squeal of brakes the train shuddered to a halt and the driver jumped out. "What's going on?"

Peter and Phyllis showed him the landslide. But not Bobbie. She had fainted and lay on the track, white and quiet as a fallen statue, still gripping her petticoat flags.

The driver picked her up and put her in one of the first class carriages. Peter and Phyllis were worried, until finally Bobbie began to cry.

"You children saved lives today," said the driver. "I expect the Railway Company will give you a reward."

"Just like real heroes and heroines," breathed Phyllis.

Chapter 4
The terrible secret

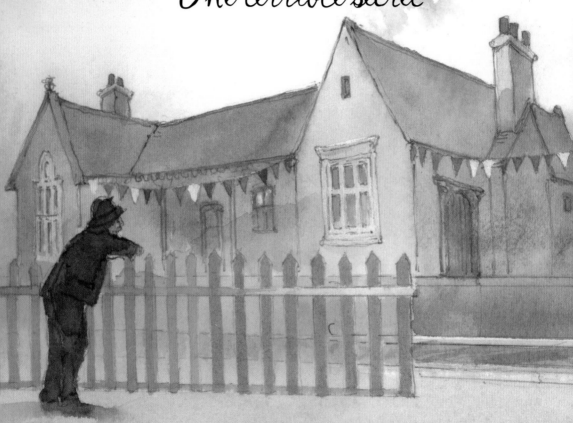

The Railway Company did want to reward the children. There was a ceremony at the station, with a brass band, decorations and cake.

All the passengers who had been on the train were there, as well as the Railway Director, the train driver, Mr. Perks, and best of all, their own old gentleman.

The Railway Director made a speech praising the children, which they found very embarrassing, and gave them each a gold watch.

When it was all over, the old gentleman shook their hands.

"Oh do come back for tea," said Phyllis.

They climbed up the hill together.
Bobbie carried the magazines Mr. Perks had collected for her. He'd made a package of them, wrapped in an old sheet of newspaper.

Back home, Mother, Phyllis and Peter chatted with the old gentleman.

Bobbie went into her room, to sort through the magazines. She undid the newspaper wrapping and idly looked at the print. Then she stared.

Her feet went icy cold and her face burned. When she had read it all, she drew a long, uneven breath.

"So now I know," she thought. It was a report of a spy trial, with a photograph of the accused. It was a photograph of Father. Underneath it said: GUILTY. And then: FIVE YEARS IN JAIL.

Bobbie scrunched up the paper. "Oh Daddy," she whispered. "You never did it."

Time passed. The old gentleman left and it grew dark outside. Supper was ready, but Bobbie couldn't join the others.

Mother came to find her.

"What's the matter?" she asked.

Bobbie held out the paper. "Tell me about it," she begged.

Mother told her how Father had been arrested for being a spy. Papers had been found in his desk that proved he had sold his country's secrets to enemies.

"Didn't they know he'd never do such a thing?" Bobbie asked.

"There was a man in his office he never quite trusted," Mother replied. "I think he planted those papers on Father."

"Why didn't you tell the lawyers that?" Bobbie wanted to know.

"Do you think I didn't try everything?" Mother demanded. "We just have to be patient and wait for him to come back to us."

"Why didn't you tell us?"

"Are you going to tell the others now you know?"

"No," said Bobbie.

"Why?"

Bobbie thought hard. "Because... it would only upset them."

"Exactly," said her mother. "But now you've found out, we must help each other to be brave."

They went in to supper together, and though Bobbie's eyes were still red with tears, Peter and Phyllis never guessed why.

Chapter 5
The man in the train

The long, cold winter blossomed into spring, and then summer. Bobbie couldn't bear the way time passed with nothing happening.

Mother was unhappy, Father was in prison, and she couldn't do anything to help. So she wrote a letter. And once more it was to the old gentleman.

Dear Friend,

Mother says we are not to ask for things for ourselves, but this isn't just for me.

You see what it says in this paper.

It isn't true. Father is not a spy.

Could you find out who did it, and then they would let Father out of prison.

Think if it was your Daddy, what would you feel? Please help me.

Love from your good friend,

Bobbie

Soon after she sent the letter, Bobbie had her twelfth birthday. Mother gave her a bracelet she no longer wore, Peter and Phyllis made a cake, and Mr. Perks brought a bunch of flowers from his garden.

It was very different from her last birthday
when she'd had a huge party and lots of
presents. This one was happy enough. But
Bobbie missed Father so badly, her mind was
filled with wanting him.

Then, one late summer's day, when the roses were out and the corn was ripening to gold, Bobbie found it impossible to concentrate on her lessons.

"Please, Mother," she begged. "Can I go outside?"

"Do you have a headache?" asked Mother.

Bobbie thought. "Not really," she replied.
"I just feel in a daze. I'd be more alive in
the fresh air, I think."

Mother let her go and Bobbie found herself
walking down to the station. She felt as if she
were in a dream.

At the station, everyone smiled at her and Mr. Perks shook her hand up and down.

"I saw it in the papers," he grinned. "I'm so pleased. And here comes the 11:54 London train, right on time."

"Saw what in the papers?" Bobbie asked, puzzled, but Mr. Perks had turned away, blowing his whistle.

As the train drew into the station, Bobbie was astonished to see handkerchiefs fluttering from every window.

Only three people got out. An old woman with a basket of squawking hens, the grocer's wife with some brown-paper packages, and the third...

"Oh! My Daddy, my Daddy!" Bobbie's cry pierced the air.

People looked out of the windows to see a tall thin man and a little girl rush up to each other with open arms.

"I felt something strange was going to happen today," said Bobbie as they walked up the hill, "but I never guessed what."

"Didn't Mother get my letter?" Father asked. "There weren't any letters this morning," Bobbie replied.

"Mother wrote to tell me you'd found out," he said. "You've been wonderful. The old gentleman has too. He helped them catch the real spy. Now, Bobbie, run ahead and tell Mother and Peter and Phyllis I'm home."

He paused in the garden, looking around at the rich summer countryside with the hungry eyes of someone who has seen too little of flowers and trees and the wide blue sky.

Mother, Bobbie, Peter and Phyllis stood in the doorway. Father went down the path to join them.

We won't follow him. In that happy moment, in that happy family, no one else is wanted just now.

The Canterville Ghost

Sir Simon
Canterville

R.I.P.

Oscar Wilde (1854-1900)

The writer Oscar Wilde was born in Ireland,
but moved to London when he was 24.
His first book, *Poems*, was published in 1881.
The Canterville Ghost was written in 1887. Wilde
also wrote fairy tales for his two sons, but he is
best known for his plays, which are still
performed today.

Chapter 1
Canterville Castle

Mr. Otis looked at the castle with delight. "I'll buy it!" he cried.

"Excellent," replied his guide, Lord Canterville. "But perhaps I should warn you... Canterville Castle is haunted."

"My family had to move out many years ago, after my great-aunt had a dreadful experience."

"She saw a skeleton. She never recovered."

Mr. Otis wasn't worried. He didn't believe in ghosts. "I'm sure my family and I will be very happy here," he smiled.

A week later, Mr. and Mrs. Otis arrived with their children, Washington, Virginia and the twins. They were greeted by an old woman, who was neatly dressed in a white apron and cap.

"I'm Mrs. Umney, the housekeeper," she said. "Come inside. There's tea for you in the library."

76

"Cake!" shouted the twins, diving in. Virginia wasn't interested in the food. She had spotted a poem in the library window.

IF A CHILD WILL ENTER THE SECRET ROOM
AND STAY TILL THE DEAD OF THE NIGHT
THEN AT LAST SIR SIMON
CAN SLEEP IN HIS TOMB
AND AT CANTERVILLE ALL WILL BE RIGHT.

Before she could show her father, Mrs. Otis cried out. "Oh dear! I'm afraid we've spilled something on the carpet, Mrs. Umney."

"It wasn't you madam," replied Mrs. Umney in a hushed voice. "*Blood* has been spilled there."

"How horrible!" cried Mrs. Otis. "It must be removed at once."

Mrs. Umney looked around nervously and began to speak in a low voice.

"It is the blood of Lady Eleanor Canterville. She was murdered on that very spot by her husband, Sir Simon Canterville, five hundred years ago."

"Seven years later, Sir Simon Canterville disappeared. His body has never been found."

Mrs. Umney's voice began to shake.
"His spirit haunts this house. That blood stain
will never go."

Washington jumped down onto the carpet
and scrubbed at the blood stain. Within
seconds, it was gone.

But as he stood up there was a crash of
thunder and a terrible flash of lightning.
 Mrs. Umney fainted.

The thunderstorm lasted the entire night.
Rain lashed at the windows and the wind
howled down the chimneys.

And next morning, in the very same spot on the library carpet, there was the blood stain.

Chapter 2
Clanking chains

"There must be a simple explanation," cried
Mr. Otis.

That night, Mr. Otis locked the library door himself and took the key to bed with him. But the blood stain still came back.

After what happened the following night, Mr. Otis thought differently about ghosts.

At midnight, he was woken by a strange noise outside his room.

It sounded like rusty chains being dragged along the ground and it seemed to be coming closer every second.

Mr. Otis was annoyed. He put on his slippers and picked up a small bottle from his bedside table. Then he opened the door...

...to a terrible sight. An old
man, with long greasy hair
and ragged clothes was
glaring at him out of
fiery red eyes.

"You must be Sir Simon," said Mr. Otis calmly. "I'm afraid, my dear sir, I must ask you to oil your chains. They make an awful noise. This bottle of oil should help."

Mr. Otis left the bottle on a table and went back to bed.

For a moment the Canterville Ghost was still. Then he smashed the bottle of oil onto the floor and fled down the corridor, howling.

The twins heard him. As Sir Simon reached the top of the stairs, they raced out of their bedroom with a pillow. Sir Simon felt a rush of air as the pillow whizzed past his head. It very nearly hit him.

The ghost quickly vanished, to appear in
his secret chamber in the west wing. He
was furious.

"I have been scaring people for hundreds
of years," he grumbled, "but never have
I been treated like this."

"How dare these newcomers give me oil for
my chains and throw pillows at my head. I must
get my revenge!"

Chapter 3
The ghost's revenge

"There's no
need to be scared
of ghosts," Mr. Otis told his family
the next morning, "but you mustn't throw
pillows at them. It's rude."

The twins grinned.

"We'll have to take those chains off him," said Mrs. Otis, "or we'll never get any sleep." But for the rest of that week there was no sign of the ghost.

The twins looked for him everywhere. They wanted to play more tricks on him.

Fresh blood stains continued to appear each morning. Strangely, each stain was a different shade. The family made guesses as to what shade it would be next.

One morning, it was even a brilliant green. When she saw that, Virginia looked cross, though she wouldn't say why.

Meanwhile, the ghost was busy plotting
his revenge. He spent days looking over his
wardrobe, deciding what to wear.

He planned to creep to
Washington's room and make
faces at the boy from the foot of his bed. Then,
he would stab himself in the neck three times to
the sound of slow music.

Sir Simon especially disliked Washington. It was Washington who kept removing the blood stains.

Virginia, on the other hand, had never been rude. "I shall only groan at her a few times from her wardrobe," he thought. "As for the twins..."

The twins, of course, deserved the worst treatment. He'd get them. He would turn into a skeleton and crawl around their beds, staring at them from one rolling eyeball.

At half-past ten the family went to bed. For a while Sir Simon heard shrieks of laughter from the twins' room, but at last all was quiet.

He crept stealthily into the corridor. An owl beat its wings against the window pane, but the Otis family slept on, peacefully unaware.

Sir Simon glided along like an evil shadow, a cruel smile stretching his wrinkled mouth. Finally, he reached the corner of the passage that led to Washington's room.

He chuckled to himself, turned the corner, then let out a wail of terror. Sir Simon fell back, hiding his face in his bony white hands.

Right in front of him was a horrible vision.
It was bald and white, with red light
streaming from its eyes. Sir Simon
had never seen another ghost
before. He was terrified.

He fled back to his room, tripping on his
sheet as he went.

Back in his chamber, he flung himself into his coffin and slammed down the lid. But as the sun rose, his bravery returned.

"I shall go and talk to the ghost," he decided. "Perhaps we can deal with the twins together. Two ghosts have got to be better than one."

By morning, the ghost looked very different. The light had gone from its eyes and it had collapsed against the wall.

Sir Simon rushed forward and seized it in his arms. To his horror, its head slipped off and rolled on the floor.

He was holding a white curtain, a broom and a large pumpkin. He had been tricked! Sir Simon ground his toothless gums together in fury, swore revenge and stomped back to his coffin.

Chapter 4
Sir Simon is upset

Sir Simon was cross and tired. The excitement of the past few days had been too much for him. For five days he stayed in his room. He even gave up making new blood stains.

With the twins constantly playing tricks on him, he only felt safe in his room. He knew it was his ghostly duty to appear in the corridor once a week, but he made sure he wasn't seen or heard.

He even slipped into Mr. Otis's bedroom and took a bottle of oil for his chains. But he still wasn't left alone.

The twins put down pins for him to tread on. One night they even stretched a piece of string across the corridor.

"That's it!" he decided. "I'm going to scare those twins one last time, if it kills me."

103

"I'll appear as my most terrifying character, Reckless Rupert the Headless Earl," he thought. Reckless Rupert always worked.

Sir Simon spent two days getting ready. Finally, he was satisfied with his appearance.

As the clock struck midnight, he made his way to the twins' bedroom. He flung open the door...

...and a large jug of icy water tipped over him. He was soaked. Sir Simon heard muffled shrieks of laughter from the twins' beds.

Furious, Sir Simon squelched back to his room. The next day he had a very bad cold. "I must give up all hope of scaring the Otis family," he said sadly.

He started creeping along the passages in his slippers.

One night he decided to creep to the library.
He wanted to see if there was any blood left on
the carpet. Suddenly, two figures jumped out at
him from the darkness.

In terror, Sir Simon
ran to the stairs. But
there was Washington
Otis, aiming a garden
hose at him.

Sir Simon vanished into the fireplace, which
– luckily for him – wasn't lit. He arrived back in
his room in a terrible state.

After that, he did not leave his room at all.
The Otis family started to think the ghost
had left.

The twins lay in wait for Sir Simon for several nights, but there was no sign of him.

"I'll write a letter to Lord Canterville," said Mr. Otis. "I'm sure he'll be interested to hear that Sir Simon has gone away at last."

Chapter 5
The secret chamber

Some weeks later, Virginia was out walking in the fields, when she tore her dress climbing through a hedge.

"I'll have to change," she thought, and decided to go up the back staircase, so she wouldn't be seen. On the way, she noticed that the door to the Tapestry Room was open.

"How odd!" she thought. "No one ever uses the Tapestry Room." Virginia peered around the door. To her surprise, she saw the Canterville Ghost.

Sir Simon was sitting by the window, his
head in his hands. He looked so upset Virginia
thought she should try and comfort him.

"Cheer up," she said. "The boys are going to school tomorrow, so the tricks will stop. Besides, if you behave yourself, no one will annoy you."

Sir Simon jumped up. "How can I behave myself?" he shouted. "I have to rattle my chains and groan through keyholes and walk around at night. I'm a ghost."

"You don't *have* to do anything," said Virginia. "What's more, you've been very wicked. Mrs. Umney told us that you murdered your wife. It's wrong to kill people,"
she pointed out.

"Yes, it was wrong," sighed Sir Simon, "but that was no reason for her brothers to starve me to death."

"Oh, poor ghost!" said Virginia. "I didn't know about that. Are you hungry now? Would you like a sandwich?"

"No thank you," he answered. "I never eat now. But it's kind of you to offer. You know," he added, "you're much nicer than the rest of your horrible family."

"How dare you be rude about my family!"
cried Virginia. "You're mean, you lie and you
stole all the paints out of my
paint box for that blood
stain. First my reds, then
the yellows – even
the greens."

"I think you should apologize," Virginia
demanded, angrily.

The ghost shrugged. "I don't see why I should. After all, what else could I do? Real blood is so hard to get hold of these days. And your brother would keep cleaning up."

"Fine," said Virginia. "If you won't apologize, I'm leaving." She turned to go.

"No, don't go," the ghost cried out.

"Please help me," Sir Simon called. "I'm so unhappy and so very, very tired."

Now Virginia was curious. "Why are you tired? Can't you sleep?"

"I haven't slept for five hundred years," Sir Simon told her.

Virginia gasped.

"And it would be so pleasant to lie in the soft brown earth," the ghost went on, "with grasses waving above my head, listening to silence..."

"Can't anyone help you?" asked Virginia.

"You could," whispered the ghost.

Virginia trembled as he spoke and a cold shudder passed through her. "How?" she asked.

"Have you ever read the poem on the library window?"

"Yes, often." Virginia thought of it now.

IF A CHILD WILL ENTER THE SECRET ROOM
AND STAY TILL THE DEAD OF THE NIGHT
THEN AT LAST SIR SIMON
CAN SLEEP IN HIS TOMB
AND AT CANTERVILLE ALL WILL BE RIGHT.

"But I don't know what it means."

"It means," said the ghost, "that you must come with me to my secret chamber and pray for me."

"That sounds easy," said Virginia.

"Mmm," said Sir Simon, "but no living person has ever entered the chamber and come out alive."

Virginia was terrified. But she did want to help. "I'll come with you, Sir Simon," she said bravely. "Lead the way."

Sir Simon took her hand in his cold, clammy fingers. Together they walked to the end of the room, where the wall disappeared before her eyes.

In a moment, the wall had closed behind them and Virginia vanished into the ghost's secret chamber.

Chapter 6
Peace at last

Ten minutes later the bell rang for tea. As Virginia did not appear, Mrs. Otis sent a footman to find her. But the footman couldn't find her anywhere.

At first Mrs. Otis thought she must be in the stables. When Virginia still hadn't returned two hours later, she began to panic.

"Boys," she called to her sons, "go and see if you can find her." But she was nowhere to be found.

Mrs. Otis even asked Mr. Otis to drain the fish pond. But there was no sign of Virginia anywhere.

At last the family sat down to supper. It was a sad meal and hardly anyone spoke. Even the twins were quiet. As the family left the dining room, the clock in the tower began to strike midnight.

On the last stroke there was a crash and a sudden, shrill cry. A panel at the top of the staircase flew back and Virginia staggered out.

Everyone rushed up to her. Mrs. Otis hugged her, Mr. Otis patted her head and the twins danced around them all.

"Where have you been?" said Mrs. Otis, rather angrily. "I've been so worried. You must not play tricks, Virginia."

"I've been with the ghost," said Virginia
quietly. "He's gone. He's been very wicked, but
he was sorry for everything he'd done. And
look! He gave me this box of jewels just before
he left."

Four days later, they held a funeral for Sir Simon. The procession left Canterville Castle at eleven o'clock at night. The carriages were drawn by four black horses, each with a great tuft of ostrich-feathers on its head.

Lord Canterville came all the way from
Wales to take part. He sat in the first carriage
with Virginia. Then came Mr. and Mrs. Otis,
followed by Washington and the twins.

It was all wonderfully impressive.

In the last carriage sat Mrs. Umney. After all, she had been frightened of the ghost for fifty years. It was only fair she should see the last of him.

The next day Mr. Otis had a word with Lord Canterville. "I think we should return the box of jewels to you. They're beautiful. Especially the ruby necklace."

"No thank you, Mr. Otis," replied Lord Canterville. "The jewels were given to Virginia for being so brave and I think she truly deserves them."

Virginia wore the ruby necklace whenever she went to a party. But, however much Washington and the twins begged, she never told anyone what happened in the secret chamber.

And Sir Simon lay in peace, at last sleeping beneath the soft earth.

The Wizard of Oz

L. Frank Baum (1856-1919)

L. Frank Baum grew up in a wealthy American family. He had several jobs before becoming a writer, including running a grocery store and breeding chickens. But he always loved telling stories – and people loved reading them. *The Wizard of Oz* was an instant hit when it was published, sparking off a whole series of books set in Oz, as well as a famous film.

Chapter 1
The cyclone

Dorothy lived on a lonely farm in Kansas, with only her Uncle Henry, her Aunt Em and her little dog Toto for company. One day, as they played outside, the sky grew dark...

Then the wind whipped up, with a
chilling moan.

"There's a cyclone coming,"
called her Uncle Henry.
"Quick, into the cellar!"

In a panic, Toto ran to hide under her bed.
Dorothy dashed after him, as the wind shrieked
and the whole house shook.

With a mighty wrench, the cyclone whirled
the house into the sky. Dorothy shivered
with terror.

"What will happen to us, Toto?"
she whispered.

The house sailed through the sky for hours...
Suddenly, with a sickening jolt, they landed.

"Welcome to Oz," cried a man in a pointed
hat, "and thank you! You've just killed the
Wicked Witch of the East and
set us free."

"Who? What?" asked Dorothy, horrified. "I
haven't killed anyone."

"Well, your house did," a woman told her.
"Look!" Two scrawny legs stuck out from under
a wall.

As Dorothy looked, the legs vanished,
leaving only a pair of silvery shoes behind.
The woman handed them to Dorothy.

"These are yours now," she said.

Dorothy took the shoes in a daze.
"Do you know the way to Kansas?"
she asked. "I have to go home."
The strangers shook their heads.
"Maybe the Great Wizard can help,"
        suggested the woman. "He lives
            in Emerald City, at the end
                of the yellow
                    brick road..."

Chapter 2
A scarecrow, a tinman and a lion

Emerald City

Dorothy packed some food and set out for the city at once. She walked briskly along the yellow road, her silver shoes tinkling on the bricks.

143

As she passed a field, a scarecrow winked at her. Dorothy jumped in surprise.

"How do you do?" he asked.

"He talks too!" thought Dorothy. "H-hello," she said, shyly. "How are you?"

"Not so good," the scarecrow said. "It's very boring stuck up here..."

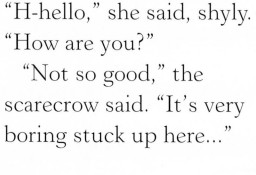

"Where are you off to?" he asked, a moment later.

"To see the wizard," Dorothy replied. "I need help to get home."

"Wizard? What wizard?" said the scarecrow. "I don't know anything," he added sadly. "I have no brains."

"Oh dear," said Dorothy. "Well, why don't you come with me? Maybe the wizard could give you some brains."

So they went on together. The land grew wilder until, by evening, they were walking through a thick forest. That night, they sheltered in a log cabin.

Dorothy woke to hear strange groans. A man made of tin was standing, as still as a statue, by a pile of logs.

"Are you alright?" she asked.

"No!" the tinman grunted. "I can't move. I was caught in the rain and I've rusted."

Dorothy spotted an oil can and swiftly oiled the tinman's joints.

"Thank you," he sighed. "I might have stood there forever. What brings you here?"

"The scarecrow and I are going to see the Great Wizard," Dorothy told him. "I want to go home and the scarecrow wants a brain."

The tinman thought for a second. "Do you think the wizard could give me a heart?" he asked.

"I expect so," said Dorothy.

"Then I'll come too," he decided.

The new companions had just set off when a lion leaped onto the road. Opening his slobbery jaws, he gave a terrible roar.

As the lion towered over Toto, Dorothy smacked him on the nose.

"Stop it!" she cried. "You must be a coward to pick on a little dog."

The lion looked ashamed. "You're right," he mumbled. "I only roar to make people run away."

"You should ask the wizard for courage," said Dorothy and told him where they were going.

The lion nodded eagerly. "I'll come with you!" he growled.

Chapter 3
A dangerous journey

The companions strolled on to the edge of
the forest, where a deep ditch barred
their way.

"We're stuck," sighed the lion.

But the scarecrow had an idea. "If the
tinman chops down this tree, we could
use it to cross the ditch."

The tree made a perfect bridge. They were almost across when they heard fierce growls from behind.

"A tiger monster!" whimpered the lion. "We're all doomed..."

"Quick, tinman!" ordered the scarecrow. "Chop away the tree."

The tree bridge fell with a crash and the
monster plummeted into the ditch. Dorothy
and her friends hurried on. Soon, they arrived at
a broad river.

"We need a raft," declared the scarecrow, and
the tinman set to work once again.

The raft bobbed along happily until they reached the middle of the river. Here, the current was so strong, it swept them away.

"We'll never reach Emerald City," wailed the lion.

Diving into the water, he took hold of the raft and swam as hard as he could. Slowly, he pulled them ashore.

Safely over the river, they went on, through a field bursting with poppies. A spicy scent filled the air and Dorothy felt drowsy. She sank into the flowers and wouldn't wake.

"It's the poppies..." yawned the lion. "They've sent... her... to sleep."

Luckily, the tinman and the scarecrow – who weren't made of flesh – stayed wide awake.

"Run!" the scarecrow ordered the lion. "We'll bring Dorothy."

The lion bounded ahead, leaving the scarecrow and tinman to carry Dorothy and Toto from the field.

On and on the pair staggered. Almost at
the end of the poppies they passed the lion
– fast asleep.

Quickly, they laid Dorothy in the open air to
recover and went back. With much pushing and
pulling, grunting and groaning, they dragged
the lion to safety.

Chapter 4
Emerald City

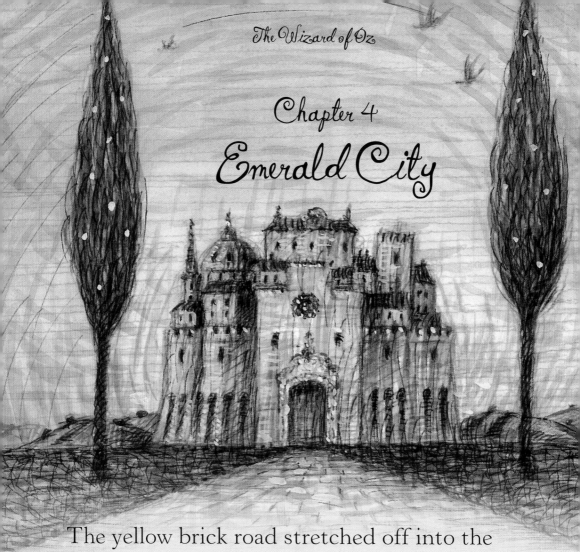

The yellow brick road stretched off into the distance, but on the horizon, something sparkled. Soon, a vast green city loomed ahead.

"We've made it!" said Dorothy.

"Look," added the lion, pointing to a gate studded with emeralds.

158

Dorothy knocked on the gate and a man in a green uniform appeared.

"Yes?" he said.

"Please may we see the Great Wizard?" asked Dorothy.

"I can take you to his palace," said the man, "but you must wear glasses. Our city is dazzling." And he pulled out a pair of green glasses for each of them, including Toto.

Inside, the city was an incredible sight. The streets and houses were built of shining green marble and all the people wore green. The shops sold green popcorn, green hats and green shoes. Everything was green – even the sky.

The gatekeeper led them to a grand palace.

"We'd like to see the wizard," Dorothy told the soldier on guard.

"Enter one at a time," he barked. "You first."

Nervously, Dorothy went inside.

"I am the wizard," boomed a giant head. "Why do you seek me?"

Dorothy took a deep breath. "Can you send me home to Kansas?"

The head frowned. "Only if you do something for me first," it snapped. "Kill the Wicked Witch of the West. Now go!"

Then the scarecrow stepped in.

A lady with green wings was sitting on the throne. "I am the wizard," she said gently. "What do you seek?"

"I am only a scarecrow, stuffed with straw. I ask you for brains."

"Kill the Wicked Witch of the West and I'll give you what you want," she murmured.

The tinman saw a terrible beast with five eyes and five limbs.

"I am the wizard," roared the beast. "Why do you seek me?"

"I am made of tin and have no heart. Please give me a heart, so I can love and be happy," he begged. But he too was turned away, with the same command.

The lion went last. Now, above the throne, blazed a ball of fire.

"I am the wizard," hissed the ball. "Why do you seek me?"

"I am a c-c-coward," stammered the lion. "I want c-c-courage, so I may truly be King of the Beasts." But the lion didn't fare any better than the others. He too was told to kill the Wicked Witch of the West.

Outside the palace, the friends were glum. "We can't defeat a witch," moaned the scarecrow.

"But we can try," said the lion. So they walked back to the gate.

"Good luck," said the gatekeeper, pointing out the path to the witch's castle. "You'll need it!"

Chapter 5
A wicked witch

The Wicked Witch of the West had only one eye, but it saw a long way. She spotted the friends as they left the city. "Strangers coming here?" she screeched. She blew a whistle and a pack of wolves ran up. "Tear the strangers to shreds," she said.

The wolves bared their teeth and dashed away.
Luckily, the tinman heard them coming.

As the first
wolf reached them,
he chopped off its head.
Again and again he swung his
hatchet, until all the wolves lay dead.

The witch scowled. She blew her whistle twice and a flock of crows flew down. "Peck the strangers to pieces," she snapped.

This time, the scarecrow saw them coming. As the first crow flew at him, the scarecrow grabbed him and wrung his neck. One by one, he wrung the neck of every single crow.

Now the witch was furious. She blew three times on her whistle to fetch a swarm of bees. "Sting the strangers to death!" she screamed.

Quickly, the scarecrow scattered straw over Dorothy, Toto and the lion to hide them. The bees tried to attack the tinman instead, but they snapped their stingers on his hard, tin body and died.

The witch gnashed her teeth, but she had one last trick up her sleeve – a cap that gave its owner three wishes. The witch had one wish left.

As she put on the cap, a crowd of magic monkeys appeared in a rush of wings. "Kill the strangers!" she howled. "Except the lion. I want him as my slave."

The monkeys flew off and seized the friends. They pulled out the scarecrow's stuffing and dropped him in the trees. They threw the tinman onto a rocky plain, smashing him to pieces. And they tied up the lion to carry him to the castle.

But at Dorothy, they stopped. "We can't hurt her," they said. "Let's take her to the witch."

Dorothy didn't know it, but the silver shoes gave her great power. The witch gulped when she saw them... until she noticed how frightened Dorothy was.

"She doesn't know about the shoes!" the witch thought gleefully. "Do as I say, or I'll kill you," she screamed at Dorothy, and set her to work.

The lion was tied up outside. Dorothy couldn't see how they'd ever escape. Every way out was guarded by the witch's slaves.

But the witch had lost much of her power. "My wolves, my crows, my bees... all dead," she thought angrily. "Even my cap has no more wishes left. I need a plan. I must steal those silver shoes."

Silently, the witch put an invisible iron bar on the ground. Dorothy tripped over it and one of her shoes flew off. The witch pounced on it.

"Give me back my shoe," said Dorothy crossly.

"Never," cackled the witch. "And I shall steal the other one too!"

Dorothy was so angry she threw a pail of water over the witch. At once, the witch began to shrink.

"Agh! I'm melting..." she wailed.

Soon, all that was left of the witch was a brown puddle and one silver shoe. Dorothy hastily put her shoe back on and raced out to the lion.

"The witch is dead!" she shouted.

Chapter 6
The wizard's trick

The witch's slaves danced with joy and helped Dorothy and the lion look for their friends. It didn't take long to find the battered remains of the scarecrow and the tinman.

The tinman was soon put back together and after the scarecrow had been stuffed with fresh straw, he felt as good as new.

"Now," said Dorothy, "let's go and claim our rewards!" So they packed her basket with food from the witch's kitchen, covered it with a cloth cap and set off.

After several hours, they stopped for lunch. "I can't wait to see the wizard," said Dorothy, as she unpacked the basket. "I wish we were in Emerald City now." Suddenly, there was a fluttering of wings and, to everyone's surprise, the magic monkeys appeared.

All at once, the friends were flying through the air. "The cloth cap must be a wishing cap," Dorothy gasped.

Before long, they could see the shining roofs of Emerald City. The monkeys set them down and flew away.

The wizard kept them waiting for ages. Finally, a soldier with a green beard ushered them in.

This time, the room was empty, but a voice echoed, "I am the wizard. Why do you seek me?"

"To claim our rewards," said the friends. "The Wicked Witch is dead."

"But..." began the voice.

"We want our rewards!" roared the lion. Toto jumped in fright and knocked over a screen in the corner...

...to reveal a little old man, with fuzzy hair and glasses.

"Who are you?" demanded the tinman, waving his hatchet.

"I'm the wizard," croaked the man. "But you can call me Oz."

"What about the head – the lady – the beast – the ball of fire?" cried the friends.

"Um, they were tricks," Oz said, sheepishly. "I'm not a real wizard. I'm not even from here. I was in a hot-air balloon that blew off-course. Since I appeared from the sky, the people thought I was a wizard."

"They asked me to rule them and I built Emerald City. Isn't it green?" Oz asked proudly. "Of course, you have to wear green-tinted glasses for the full effect," he admitted.

"The witches were my only fear. I was so glad when your house killed the first one. I would have said anything to get rid of the other."

"But what about our rewards?" asked the friends together.

"You don't need them," Oz replied. "Scarecrow, you're full of ideas. Lion, you're brave, you just lack confidence. And Tinman, hearts make most people unhappy."

"But you promised!" they said.

Oz sighed. "I'll do my best."

"And can you send me home?" Dorothy asked.

"I'll try," Oz replied.

Chapter 7
Oz's rewards

Oz summoned everyone the very next day. "Scarecrow first," he said.

He took the scarecrow's head and tipped in a handful of pins. "This will make you as sharp as a pin!"

And the scarecrow felt very wise.

Next came the tinman. "Here's your heart," said Oz, giving him a heart-shaped cushion. "It's a very kind one." The tinman beamed.

Then Oz produced a green bottle. "This is courage," he told the lion.

The lion gulped it down. "Now I feel brave!" he roared.

Finally, Oz led
Dorothy to a basket.
"I mended my balloon,"
he said.
"We'll
fly home!"

He lit a fire and hot air swelled the balloon.
The basket began to lift.

"Hurry!" Oz cried to Dorothy – but she was
looking for Toto. She swept him up and ran to
the basket.

189

Just as she reached it, a rope snapped and the balloon took off.

"Come back!" she called. It was too late. "Now I'll never get home," she wept. Her friends hated to see her so unhappy. The scarecrow racked his new brains.

"I know," he said. "Wish for the magic monkeys to take you!"

But they couldn't help. "We can't leave this land," they explained.

Then a soldier spoke up. "Why not ask the Good Witch Glinda?"

So Dorothy and her friends set off once more.

Chapter 8
Home again

Glinda lived far in the south. It would have been a difficult journey without the cap's third wish.

"Please take us to Glinda," said Dorothy and the monkeys carried them to a beautiful castle.

"What can I do for you?" Glinda asked her visitors kindly.

Dorothy told her the whole story. "And now I just want to go home," she finished.

"Bless you," said Glinda, smiling. "I'm sure I can get you all home. But I'll need the wishing cap."

She turned to the others. "What will you do when Dorothy leaves?"

"I'll live in Emerald City," the scarecrow told her.

"I'll go back to my cabin," said the tinman.

"And I'll go home to the forest," added the lion.

"I'll ask the monkeys to take you all where you wish," said Glinda. "Then I'll set them free."

"You're very kind," said Dorothy, "but please, how can I get home?"

"Your silver shoes will take you," replied Glinda. "Just knock the heels together three times and say where you want to go."

With glistening eyes, Dorothy said goodbye to her friends. Then she hugged Toto tightly and clicked her heels together.

"Take me home!" she cried.

At once, she was whirling through the air... and rolling on the soft grass of a familiar field.

Aunt Em dropped her watering can and rushed over. "My darling child!" she said, covering Dorothy with kisses. "Wherever did you come from?"

"From Oz," said Dorothy. "And oh, Aunt Em, I'm so glad to be home!"

198

Black Beauty

Anna Sewell (1820-1878)

Anna Sewell adored horses. She suffered from a bone disease and, after spraining her ankle as a young girl, she became increasingly lame. For the last six years of her life, she couldn't move from her house. She longed to make people more caring about horses, so she wrote *Black Beauty* (her only book), lying on her sofa. Anna died just after it was published, never knowing its success.

Chapter 1
In the beginning

When I was very young my life was gloriously happy. I galloped with other colts by day and slept by my mother's side at night.

But when I was four years old, a man named Squire Gordon came to talk to my master, the horse breeder.

He stroked my black coat and the white star on my forehead. "Beautiful!" he exclaimed. "Break him in and I'll buy him!"

Then he touched the white patch on my back.
"It's like a beauty spot," he said. "I'll call him
Black Beauty."

I shook with fear. I was going to be sold!
Would I have to leave my mother? And
what was *breaking in*?

"You must learn to wear a saddle and bridle," my mother explained. Then the groom thrust a cold steel bar into my mouth and held it there, with straps over my head and under my throat. There was no escape.

At first the bar frightened me, but with kind words and treats of oats I learned to get used to it.

Just before I was taken to Squire Gordon, my mother spoke to me for the last time. "Now, Black Beauty," she whispered, "be brave. All young horses must leave their mothers to make their way in the world."

"Just remember – never bite or rear or kick. And whatever happens, always do your best."

When Squire Gordon's groom arrived, he
jumped on my back and we rode away.
I cantered through twisting villages
until we reached a long drive.
Apple orchards stretched out
on either side.

The groom led me into a large, airy stable
with plenty of corn and hay. A friendly whinny
from the next stall made me look up.

A fat little pony with a thick mane and tail was poking his head over the rail. "I'm Merrylegs," he said. "Welcome to Birtwick Park."

"That was John who rode you here," Merrylegs went on. "He's the best groom around – and Squire Gordon is the best owner a horse could have. You'll be happy here."

A tall chestnut mare glared at Merrylegs. "Trouble is, no one knows how long a good home will last," she snapped. "I've had more homes than you've had hot oats."

"Meet Ginger," said Merrylegs. "She bites. That's why she keeps getting sold, even though she's so handsome."

Angrily, Ginger tore at wisps of hay in her manger. "You don't know anything," she muttered. "If you'd been through what I have, you'd bite too."

"Poor Ginger!" I thought. "What could have made her so unhappy?"

Chapter 2
Ginger's story

Over the next few days, John took me out. At first we went slowly... then we trotted and cantered, and ended up in a wonderful speedy gallop.

"Well, John, how is my new horse?" asked Squire Gordon.

"First rate, Sir," replied John, grooming me carefully. "Black Beauty's as swift as a deer, as gentle as a dove and as safe as houses."

"A lady's horse, perhaps?" asked the Squire's wife, feeding me pieces of apple.

"Oh yes, Mrs. Gordon. He'll be a good carriage horse too. We could try him out with Ginger," John suggested.

So I was paired up with Ginger to pull the carriage. During our journeys, she told me the story of her life.

"If I'd had your upbringing, I might be good tempered like you," she began. "My first memory is of a stone being thrown at me."

"Poor you!" I said, but Ginger hadn't finished. "When my first owner broke me in, he shoved a painful bit in my mouth," she went on.

"I reared up in pain and he fought me with his whip until blood poured from my flanks...

...and then he cut off my tail."

"Why?" I cried. I'd noticed Ginger had
no tail, but thought she must have lost it in
an accident.

"Fashion," Ginger replied bitterly. "Some
people think horses look better with a stump.
Now I have nothing to whisk flies away with."

She sighed. "It's agony when they crawl on me and sting."

"Horrible!" I snorted.

"That's not all. My first owner sold me to a rich London gentleman who put me in a bearing rein."

"A what?" I asked.

"It's a tight rein that pulls your neck all the way back. Imagine your tongue pinched, your jaw jerked upright and your neck on fire with pain.

Everyone thought I looked wonderful, but oh, how it hurt! Kindness wins us, not painful whips," said Ginger.

"But we're lucky here," she said, at last. "Squire Gordon hates bearing reins, and John is teaching young Joe, our new groom, to be just as good as he is.

And I'm *trying* to behave now, because everyone's so kind."

Chapter 3
Horses know best

Soon after this, Mrs. Gordon fell ill. We didn't see her for weeks. Then one stormy night John rushed to the stables.

"Best foot forward, Beauty," he cried. "We must ride as hard as we can to fetch the doctor. Mrs. Gordon is at death's door."

We galloped into lashing rain, while thunder and lightning raged around us.

Leaves and twigs danced in the air, torn from their branches by a savage wind.

As we got to the main road, a terrible splitting sound crashed through the darkness. A huge tree had fallen in our path.

Gathering all my strength, I jumped – and sailed over it.

At last we reached the bridge. I could hear the river roaring. But the moment I stepped onto the bridge, I stopped.

"Come on, Beauty," John urged.

I couldn't move. I could tell something was wrong. John gave me a light touch of the whip, but I stayed like a statue.

Just then, the moon lit up the bridge. We saw the far end had collapsed into matchsticks, tossing in the raging water.

"Well done, Beauty!" John cried. "We would have been killed. But I'm afraid it's ten miles to the next bridge. We'll have to hurry."

"Gallop and get there…" I murmured to myself. "Gallop and get there…" The faster I said it, the faster I went.

I raced home with both John and the doctor on my back. I'd never been so tired in my life.

"You're steaming like a kettle," said young Joe. "You're too hot for your blanket. Here, have some ice-cold water."

All through the night I shivered and sweated and longed for John to come. When he arrived, he was horrified. "Joe! You've nearly killed Beauty!" he shouted. "He's caught a bad chill.

You should have put on his blanket — and that icy drink did him no good at all."

"I didn't know," Joe muttered sulkily.

"Didn't know?" yelled John. "You should make it your business to know. If you don't know, ask!"

"I'm sorry," wept Joe. "I didn't mean to hurt him. Will he die?"

"Let's hope not," replied John.

With careful nursing, I recovered, but Joe never forgot the lesson he had learned.

Chapter 4
A terrible time

Mrs. Gordon got better too, but the doctor said she must live in the sun to be really well.

Everything was to be sold – Birtwick Park, Merrylegs, Ginger and me. Merrylegs went to the priest, who'd promised to keep him for good.

We said goodbye under the apple trees, where we'd talked and played so happily. I never saw Merrylegs again.

Ginger and I were sold to Lord and Lady Richmore. John had tears in his eyes when he handed us over to Reuben, our new groom.

The next day, Lord and Lady
Richmore came to inspect us.

"They look very nice, Reuben," announced
Lady Richmore. "They can pull my carriage.
But you must put their heads up. High."

"Squire Gordon never used a bearing rein," Lord Richmore reminded her.

"Well, I won't have horrible, common-looking horses," snapped Lady Richmore.

Reuben pulled my head back and fixed the rein tight. I felt red-hot pain. Ginger tried to jerk her head away, but Reuben forced her rein like mine.

Instantly, I saw why Ginger hated it. I couldn't put my head down to take the strain of pulling the carriage. As the strength drained out of us, Reuben whipped us on.

At last, we came to a
grand courtyard crammed
with horses and carriages.
Ginger couldn't take it
any more.

With a wild neigh she reared up, scaring all
the horses who crashed into each other, kicking
madly. Our carriage toppled over and broke
to pieces.

Lady Richmore tumbled out, unharmed but furious.

Ginger was taken away forever. I longed to know what happened to her, but no one mentioned her name again.

I didn't trust Reuben. He oozed politeness to the Richmores, but secretly he drank too much.

One evening, he took me out for a ride on a road made of fresh-laid sharp stones. My shoe was loose, but Reuben was too drunk to notice.

He never heard the clatter of my shoe falling
off. I don't think he even noticed me limping.
My hoof split and – I couldn't help it! I fell onto
my knees. Reuben shot to the ground, hit his
head on the cobbles and lay there,
not moving.

I stayed with Reuben all through the night.
When morning dawned, a group of early walkers
came by. They were shocked at the sight of us.

"That's Reuben," they shouted. "Dead, poor
bloke. Thrown by that horse! Vicious brute!
That'll be the end of him."

No one knew what really happened. And what
would they do to me now?

Chapter 5
Life is a puzzle

"I'm going to sell that bad-tempered Black Beauty to any fool who wants him," Lord Richmore announced.

I was sorry for Reuben, but I couldn't help being thrilled to be leaving Lord and Lady Richmore.

I was put into a horse sale. Buyers prodded me and stared at me, but no one wanted me.

"Isn't he ugly with those nasty knees?" I heard someone say.

Finally a kind-looking man paid a small sum of money for me and took me away.

The man's name was Jerry Barker and he lived
in London with his wife and children – Harry
and the twins, Polly and Molly.

"I want you to be my cab horse," Jerry told
me. "I'll call you Jack."

It was strange to have a new name. My job was to be harnessed to Jerry's carriage, which he called his cab, and pick up passengers when they hailed us in the street.

We worked hard, out all day in all weather – rain, sleet, snow and ice – with hardly any rest.

I didn't mind anything because Jerry was such a kind, honest man. I wanted to do my best for him.

He made sure I was always comfortable and had plenty of food. He never whipped me to go faster, even if customers in a hurry bribed him with extra cash.

"You'll never be rich!" the other cab drivers jeered.

"I have enough, thanks," Jerry replied. "It's not fair on Jack to make him hurry all the time."

Other cab horses weren't so lucky. I often saw them exhausted and miserable, made old before their time with too much work.

Once I saw an old, worn-out chestnut, with a thin neck and bones that stuck out through a badly-kept coat. Its eyes had a dull, hopeless look.

I was wondering why the horse looked faintly familiar when I heard a whisper.

"Black Beauty, is that you?"

It was Ginger! Her beautiful looks had completely vanished.

She told me she belonged to a cruel driver who whipped her, starved her and overworked her.

"You used to stand up for yourself if people were mean to you," I said.

"Yes, I did once, but now I'm too tired," she replied. "I just wish I could die."

"No, Ginger!" I cried. "Keep going! Better times will come."

"I hope they do for you, Black Beauty," she whispered. "Goodbye and good luck."

Soon after that meeting I saw a cart carrying a dead chestnut horse. It was a dreadful sight.

I think it was Ginger. I almost hope it was, for that meant her suffering was over.

Chapter 6
An unexpected ending

One day, a customer of Jerry's made him an
offer he couldn't refuse. She asked him to be her
groom at her house in the country.

"There's a little cottage for you and your family," she said. "I wish I could take Jack too, but I already have a horse."

"Sorry, old Jack," Jerry comforted me. "I hope someone kind will buy you."

But my new master was a cruel man. I
had to pull his carts loaded with sacks of corn,
and if I was too slow, he whipped me hard. He
hardly fed me either, which made me weak.

In the end I simply collapsed in the street.
"Stupid horse!" my master grunted. "Is he
dead? What a waste of money."

I couldn't move. As I lay there barely breathing, someone came up and poured water down my throat. A gentle voice said, "He's not dead, only exhausted."

The gentle voice belonged to a horse doctor. I couldn't believe my luck! The doctor helped me to my feet, and led me to his stables, where he gave me a warm mash.

"I think you were a good horse once," said the doctor, "though you're a poor, broken-down old thing now. I'm going to feed you up and find you a nice home."

Rest, good food and gentle exercise worked on me like magic. But when the doctor said I was ready to leave him, I trembled all over. I dreaded to think what my next home would be like.

The doctor took me to a pretty house in a small village. It had a pasture and a comfortable stable, and belonged to two grown-up sisters, Claire and Elspeth Lyefield.

"I'm sure we'll like you," they said, patting me. "You have such a gentle face." I nuzzled them, but I wasn't sure I could trust them.

Their groom led me to the stable and began to clean me. "That white star is just like Black Beauty's," he said, "and the glossy black coat. He's about the same height too. I wonder where Black Beauty is now?"

Soon he came to the tiny knot of white hair on my back. "That's what Squire Gordon called Beauty's patch. It is Black Beauty! It really is! Do you remember me? Young Joe who nearly killed you?"

I was so glad to see him! I've never seen a man so happy, either.

I've been here now for a year. Joe is always gentle, Claire and Elspeth are kind, and my work is easy. All my strength has come back and I've never been happier.

The sisters have promised never to sell me. Finally I've found my home, for ever and ever.

The Secret Garden

Frances Hodgson Burnett (1849-1924)

Born in England in 1849, Frances moved to America with her family when she was 16. A year later, Frances sold her first story. She went on to become one of the most famous children's writers of all time. Her other books include *A Little Princess* and *Little Lord Fauntleroy*.

Chapter 1
Contrary Mary

In the scorching heat of a garden in India, Mary Lennox stamped her foot. "Fetch me a drink NOW!" she ordered.

265

Instantly, servants rushed to obey.
Meanwhile, Mary began to make a pretend
garden, sticking flowers into the hot dry earth.
"It looks all wrong," she muttered.

Glancing up, Mary saw a beautiful woman
strolling past, surrounded by an admiring group
of army officers.

"Mother!" cried Mary. She rushed forward, but Mrs. Lennox brushed her daughter away, as she always did.

It was Mary's last glimpse of her mother. Over the next few days a terrible fever, cholera, swept through her parents' house.

Her mother and father died, along with many of their servants.

Mary, shut away in the nursery, never caught the cholera. But she was left all alone in the world.

After that, Mary was passed around like a package between her parents' friends, until a letter came from her uncle, Mr. Craven.

> Misselthwaite Manor,
> Yorkshire, England
>
> Dear Mary,
>
> I have made arrangements for you to come to England and live at Misselthwaite Manor. My housekeeper, Mrs. Medlock, will meet you in London and escort you here.
>
> I'm afraid I won't see you for some time as I have to travel to Europe on business.
>
> Yours sincerely,
>
> Archibald Craven

"No one cares what I want," Mary thought, but she had nowhere else to go.

Chapter 2
The strange house

Several weeks later, Mary was sitting in a freezing cold carriage, opposite the stern-looking Mrs. Medlock.

"What's that whooshing noise?" Mary asked, as they drove across a bleak landscape.

"It's the wind howling across the moor," Mrs. Medlock replied.

"What's a moor?" asked Mary.

"Miles of empty land – and the manor is right in the middle of it."

"I hate it already," thought Mary.

271

"How many servants will I have?" she asked.

Mrs. Medlock looked shocked. "I don't know how it was in India," she said, "but here you'll take care of yourself."

They arrived late at night. Mrs. Medlock marched Mary across a huge hall, up steep stairs and along twisting corridors.

"Your bedroom," she announced, at last,
flinging open a door. "You must stay here,
unless you're going outside. On no account
must you go poking around the house."

As soon as Mary stepped into the room, Mrs.
Medlock left, shutting the door behind her
before hurrying off.

Mary looked around. It was not a child's room. Tapestries hung on the walls and in the middle stood a vast four-poster bed.

Outside the wind howled like a lonely person,
as lonely as Mary. Then another noise pierced
the wind – a far-off sobbing sound.

"That's not the wind," Mary thought. "It's a child crying. Who is it?"

She was itching with curiosity, but she didn't dare disobey Mrs. Medlock. Finally, worn out from her journey, she fell asleep.

Chapter 3
A robin and a key

The next morning, Mrs. Medlock bustled into Mary's room with her breakfast.

"Ugh!" exclaimed Mary, looking at the porridge. "What's that? It looks disgusting. I won't eat it."

277

Mrs. Medlock sighed at the pale, skinny child, swamped by the big bed. "Just drink your milk then," she said, "and you can go out."

"Don't want to," retorted Mary.

"Well, if you don't, you'll be stuck in here and there's nothing to do inside," snapped Mrs. Medlock.

Mary took a while to get dressed – she'd always had servants to dress her before – but finally she was ready.

Mrs. Medlock showed her the way to the gardens and she wandered out, past wide lawns, wintry flower beds and trees clipped into strange shapes.

The only person she could see was an old man digging.

"Who are you?" demanded Mary.

"Ben Weatherstaff," he growled.

"What's in there?" Mary asked, pointing to a crumbling, ivy-covered wall behind them.

"Ah," said Ben. "That's the secret garden. Mr. Craven shut it up."

"Why?" asked Mary.

Ben looked sad. "It was Mrs. Craven's special garden and she loved it. But she died and the master was so unhappy, he buried the key and went away."

As he spoke, a robin flew up to Ben. His wrinkled face creased into a smile.

"There's no door," Ben went on, "but that doesn't stop this one."

The robin cocked its head to the side and looked at Mary. Enchanted, she whispered, "Will you be friends with me?"

"So..." Ben murmured. "You can be friendly, after all. You sound just like Dickon talking to his animals."

"Who's Dickon?" asked Mary.

"He's the brother of a maid here," said Ben. "Dickon can grow flowers out of stones and charm the birds. Even the deer love young Dickon."

"I wish I could meet him!"

But Ben was growing impatient. "Run along now," he said. "I've got work to do."

The robin flew off. Mary followed him. "Please, robin, show me the way to the garden," she begged.

The robin chirruped and hopped up and down on the ground.

"He's telling me something," thought Mary. She scrabbled in the soil and saw, half-hidden, a rusty ring. Picking it up, she saw it wasn't a ring at all. It was a key. The key to the secret garden.

Chapter 4
Dickon

Every morning, Mary jumped out of bed, ready to search for a way into the garden.

"I have the key," she told herself. "I just need to find the door."

Mrs. Medlock noticed a change in her. "She looks downright pretty now, with her rosy cheeks," she thought. "She was so plain and scrawny at first."

One day, as the winter trees were beginning to blossom and the wind came in sweet-scented gusts from the moor, the robin fluttered down and hopped along beside Mary.

Mary never knew if what happened next was magic. A gust of wind lifted up a patch of ivy to reveal an old wooden door. Mary put her key in the lock, turned it with both hands and pushed. Slowly, the door creaked open...

She was inside the secret garden!

It was a mysterious place – a hazy, frosty tangle of rose branches that trailed the walls and spread along the ground.

Hundreds of green spiky shoots thrust up through withered grass.

"It isn't completely dead," she whispered. "I am glad."

The shoots looked so crowded that she began to clear spaces around them. The robin chirped, as though pleased someone was gardening here at last.

Mary worked for hours. "It must be lunchtime," she thought, hungrily. "I'd better go in, before Mrs. Medlock starts looking for me."

Racing back after lunch, she noticed Ben talking to a curly-haired boy, with a fawn by his side. As the boy walked away, he played a tune on a rough wooden pipe.

Shyly, Mary went up to him. "Are you Dickon?"

"I am," he grinned. "And you're Mary. Ben told me about you."

He looked so friendly and kind, Mary felt she could trust him. "Can you keep a secret?"

Dickon chuckled. "I keep secrets all the time. If I told where wild animals live and birds make their nests, they wouldn't be safe."

"I've found the secret garden," she said quickly.

"I think it's mostly dead. I'm the only person who wants it to live. Come and see."

She led him through the ivy curtain and Dickon looked around, amazed. "I never thought I'd see this place," he murmured. "It's like being in a dream."

He scraped a rose branch with his pocket knife. "There's green underneath," he said. "These roses are alive. Some dead wood needs cutting, that's all."

Mary danced around the garden in delight.

"It'll be a fountain of roses, come summer," said Dickon. "We'll add more plants too – snapdragons, larkspur, love-in-a-mist. We'll have the prettiest garden in England."

"Will you really help?" asked Mary. She could hardly believe it.

"Of course," he replied. "It's fun, shut in here, waking up a garden."

Chapter 5
A cry in the night

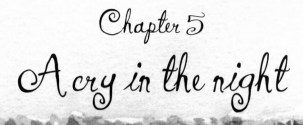

Every day they worked in the garden.

"I don't want it too tidy," Mary decided. "It wouldn't feel like a secret garden then."

"It's secret, sure enough," said Dickon. "Look – the robin's building a nest. He wouldn't do that, unless he felt safe."

"I feel safe and happy here, too," Mary confided. "But I used to be angry all the time. Nobody liked me."

Dickon's fawn nuzzled Mary's hand and he laughed. "There's someone who likes you," he said. "So does the robin and so do I."

That night, lying in bed, Mary heard the wind rage.

"I don't hate it now," she realized.

She thought of the wild animals on the moor, snuggled in their holes, protected from its blasts.

Suddenly, she was alert, listening.

"There's that noise again," she thought. "Crying. It's definitely not the wind. Where's it coming from?"

Gripping her bedside candle, she followed
the sound down shadowy passages, until she
reached a door with a glimmer of light beneath.

Quietly, she opened the door. A fire burning in the grate threw a dim light onto a huge carved bed. In the bed was a boy, sobbing. Dark eyes stared from an ivory-white face.

"Are you a ghost?" he whimpered.

"No," said Mary. "Are you?"

"I'm Colin Craven," said the boy.

Mary gasped. "Mr. Craven's my uncle. I'm Mary Lennox."

"Well, Mr. Craven's my father," said Colin.

Mary looked at him in astonishment. "Why didn't Mrs. Medlock tell me about you?"

"I don't let people talk about me," Colin said, "because I'm going to die."

Mary was horrified. "What's wrong with you?"
Colin sighed. "I'm weak."
"You won't die from that," Mary scoffed.

"And my father doesn't even care," Colin went
on, as if he hadn't heard. "He hates me because
my mother died when I was born. He can't bear
to look at me."

"Just like the secret garden," Mary said.
"What garden?"
"Your mother's garden," Mary explained.
"Your father shut it up after she died."

"I'll have it unlocked,"
Colin announced grandly.
"No!" cried Mary.
"Why not?"

"Then *everyone* would go in it. It wouldn't be a secret any more!"

"Never mind," said Colin, fretfully. "I'll never see it anyway."

"Yes you will!" argued Mary. "You go outside, don't you?"

"Never," said Colin. "I can't cope with cold air. Don't forget I'm dying."

Mary felt he was rather proud of this and she didn't like it. "Don't talk about death all the time," she said. "Think of other things."

Her voice dropped to a whisper. "Think of the sun and rain and buds bursting into flower. Think of new green leaves. Think of the secret garden, coming alive…"

Gradually, Colin's eyes closed, and Mary crept away.

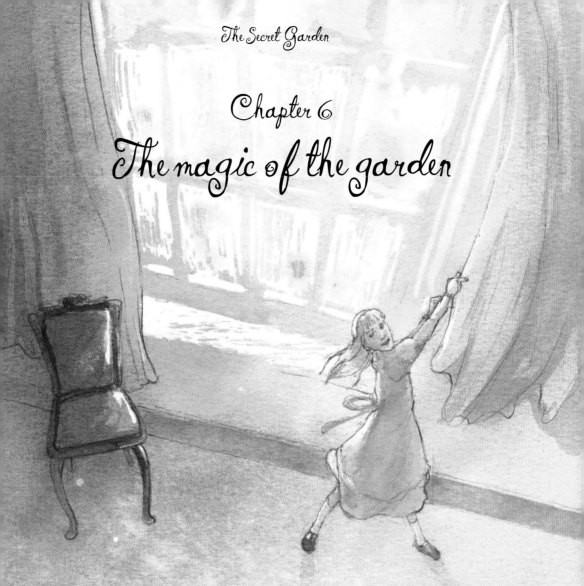

Chapter 6
The magic of the garden

The next morning Mary had to see if she'd dreamed it all. She burst into Colin's room and pulled back the curtains, flooding the room with sunlight.

Colin sat up in bed and smiled. "I've just realized," he said. "We're cousins!"

They were talking so loudly they didn't hear Mrs. Medlock come in.

"I told you not to go poking around," she shouted at Mary. "Go back to your room at once."

"No," Colin ordered. "I like her. I want her to stay with me."

"She'll tire you out," said Mrs. Medlock. "Come along, Mary."

"DO WHAT I SAY!" screamed Colin. "Leave Mary and get out."

"Yes, dear," said Mrs. Medlock, trying to sound soothing. She'd promised Mr. Craven she would never upset Colin. Hurriedly, she withdrew.

"You're horribly bossy," said Mary. "I used to be like that, when I lived in India. But I'm trying to change now."

"Why shouldn't I give orders?" snapped Colin. "I'm master of this house when Father's away." Mary got up to leave.

"Don't go!" pleaded Colin, all trace of bossiness gone from his voice.

"I don't want to be alone."

"I'll be back later," Mary promised. "I have a friend I want you to meet."

A few hours later, Mary and Dickon crept into Colin's room.

"You've been ages," complained Colin, scowling at them.

"Say hello to Dickon," said Mary. "I want you to come out with us. I want to show you a secret."

"The garden?" guessed Colin.

Mary nodded.

"I'll come," he decided and rang a bell to summon Mrs. Medlock.

"I'm going outside," he stated. "Bring my wheelchair. And tell everyone to keep away."

"Are you sure, dear?" she asked, anxiously. "You'll catch cold."

"Just do as I say," Colin ordered.

Dickon pushed Colin along the paths until Mary stopped and, flinging back the ivy, opened the garden door.

Sunshine lit up sprays of flowers and the air was alive with birdsong.

Colin stared. "I can *feel* things growing," he gasped.

"It's spring," said Dickon. "Makes you feel good. We'll soon have you working in the garden."

"But I can't even stand," Colin faltered,
looking at his thin legs.

"Only because you haven't tried," said Mary.

Dickon helped Colin to his feet.

"Try now, Colin. You can walk, you really can,"
urged Mary.

Unsteadily and clinging to Dickon, Colin forced his weak limbs to move. The others saw his pale face grow rosy in the sunlight.

"Mary! Dickon!" he cried. "I'm going to get well. I can feel it."

Chapter 7
Mr. Craven comes home

Every day they played and worked in the garden and, every day, Colin grew stronger.

By the time spring turned into summer, he was completely well. But the three of them pretended he was still ill.

"No one must know," Colin insisted. "I want to surprise my father. If only he'd come home..."

Colin began to wish, "Come home, come home."

320

One night, Colin's father, far away in Italy, had a strange dream. He heard his dead wife calling his name.

"Where are you?" he pleaded.

"In the garden," came the reply, like the sound from a golden flute.

Mr. Craven woke, determined to return to his manor at once.

"Where's Colin?" he demanded, the minute he arrived home.

Mrs. Medlock gasped, shocked at his sudden appearance.

"He plays in the garden, sir, with Mary and Dickon," she said in a shaky voice. "No one is allowed near them."

"In the garden?" thought Mr. Craven. "My dream…"

As he hurried down the path, he heard children laughing in his wife's old garden.

"The door's locked and the key's buried," he told himself. "I must still be dreaming."

Suddenly, the door burst open and Colin and Mary dashed out.

"Father! You're here!" cried Colin.

Mr. Craven hugged his son tight. "Is it really you? You're well! However did it happen?"

"It was the garden," said Colin. "And Mary."

"I thought the garden would be dead," murmured his father.

"It came alive," said Mary.

Mr. Craven smiled. "And so has Colin," he said. "Thank you, Mary."

Around the World in Eighty Days

Jules Verne (1828-1905)

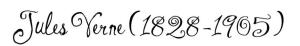

Jules Verne was a French writer who loved
science and travel, and combined them
with adventure in his stories.
His first book, *Five Weeks in a Balloon*, was
published in 1863. Ten years later, he wrote
Around the World in Eighty Days. Another of
his famous stories is *Twenty Thousand Leagues
Under the Sea*.

Chapter 1
The journey begins

Over one hundred years ago, there lived a man named Phileas Fogg. For many years, he led a very quiet life. He spent every day at his club, which was where rich men went to meet their friends.

Every morning, he left his house at exactly 11:30 and walked 576 steps to his club. Then he ate lunch.

After lunch, Fogg read three newspapers from cover to cover. Then he ate supper. After that, he played cards with friends. He won most of the rounds.

On the stroke of midnight, he went home to bed... before doing exactly the same the very next day.

But one Wednesday, everything changed. Fogg read some amazing news in his paper.

"Listen to this," he announced to his friends. "It says it's possible to travel around the world in only eighty days!"

"Surely not!" one of his friends declared.

"I'd like to see *you* do it!" said the other.

Despite his friends' laughter, Fogg was convinced he *could* do it.

332

"I will bet twenty thousand pounds that I can go around the world in eighty days or less!"

Everyone thought he was crazy, but Fogg had made up his mind.

"I shall be back on December 21st," he declared confidently, turning to leave.

As soon as he arrived home, Fogg asked Passepartout, his butler, to pack a small bag. Luckily, Passepartout had been an acrobat and could move quickly.

In less than ten minutes, they were on their way to the station...

...and at 8:45 exactly, the train pulled out. Fogg and Passepartout were off on their great adventure.

They were heading for the coast, where they could catch a boat to France. But they were also heading straight for trouble.

Chapter 2
Arriving in Africa

While Phileas Fogg was crossing Europe,
the police were hunting a runaway thief.
Only a few days before, he had stolen the
huge sum of fifty-five thousand pounds from
the Bank of England.

An inspector named Fix was convinced the thief would escape by sailing from Europe to Africa. He was waiting on the quay when Fogg reached Suez in North Africa.

Fogg sent Passepartout to get his passport stamped. "I need proof of the trip," he explained.

Quite by chance, Passepartout happened to ask Inspector Fix which was the way to the passport office.

When Fix saw the passport, he gasped. Fogg's description exactly matched the description of the thief. Fix was certain he'd found his man.

But he couldn't act at once. First, he needed some papers, which would allow him to arrest the thief.

So, Fix found out where Fogg was going and sent an urgent message to London. "Am on the trail of the thief. Following him to India. Send arrest papers to Bombay."

Fix quickly packed a small bag and boarded the ship for India.

The voyage was rough, but Fogg stayed as calm as ever. He ate four meals a day and played cards. He might have been at home.

Two days early, the ship steamed into Bombay. Inspector Fix was ready to make his arrest, but the papers had not arrived.

"My only hope," Fix decided, "is to stop Fogg from leaving India." Later that day, he saw his chance.

Passepartout had visited a temple, but he didn't realize he was supposed to take off his shoes. When a priest tugged them from his feet, he started a fight.

Fix was delighted. "Now I've seen that butler break the law, I can make sure he's arrested and jailed here – along with his master!"

Fix followed Passepartout to the station and watched him catch a train. "See you in Calcutta," Fix muttered to himself. "I'll get your Mr. Fogg there."

Chapter 3
Fogg to the rescue

The train puffed its way through India, passing magnificent temples and fields of coffee and cotton. Passepartout saw it all, amazed. Fogg found a man to play cards.

343

But halfway through the third day, the train came to a stop.

"The track ends here," a guard announced. "It starts again in fifty miles at Allahabad."

Passepartout was furious. "How will we reach Calcutta in time?" he demanded.

Fogg didn't seem worried. "I've allowed time for delays," he said quietly. "We simply need to find another way to travel."

Passepartout rushed off. Soon, he was back with the answer

— an elephant.

The elephant was expensive, but Fogg didn't mind. He invited his card-playing friend to join them.

Then he hired a guide and, half an hour later, they were lurching through the jungle. Passepartout bounced up and down with glee. Every now and then, he tossed the elephant a sugar lump.

They journeyed for hours, crossing forests of date trees and sandy plains. That night, they camped in a ruined bungalow.

They were off again at six the next morning, breakfasting on bananas picked from a tree. They had almost crossed a thick forest, when they heard music and voices. A large procession was snaking its way through the trees.

In the middle of the procession, a group of warriors carried the body of a dead prince. Behind them, two priests were pulling a beautiful girl.

Passepartout was shocked. "What are they doing?" he cried.

"It's the custom," their guide explained. "When a prince dies, his wife must die too, so they can go to heaven together."

"Tomorrow, Princess Aouda will be burned to death beside her husband."

Passepartout was horrified. Even Phileas Fogg, who let nothing disturb him, seemed upset.

"I have twelve hours to spare," he observed. "Let's save her."

By nightfall, the procession had reached a small temple. The princess was locked firmly inside.

Everything seemed hopeless, until Passepartout had an idea...

The next morning, Princess Aouda was laid beside her husband. Then the priests lit a huge fire, watched by a silent crowd. Suddenly, the air filled with screams. Some people even flung themselves to the ground. The dead prince was sitting up.

His ghostly figure rose through the smoke and grasped Princess Aouda in his arms. Then he strode off into the jungle.

"Let's go!" the ghost called to Fogg. It was Passepartout, who had disguised himself as the prince. Fogg and his friend chased after them, dodging bullets and arrows as they ran to safety.

Chapter 4
Tricked!

At Allahabad, Fogg gave the elephant to their guide and jumped on a train. But Fix had reported Passepartout's fight at the temple. As they arrived in Calcutta, Fogg and Passepartout were grabbed by police and taken to court.

Fogg and Passepartout faced a week in jail. The poor butler felt terrible. Then Fogg offered the court two thousand pounds.

"Very well," said the judge. "You may go free for now. But we'll keep the money if you don't return."

Fogg caught his next ship, to Hong Kong, with an hour to spare.

Fix was furious. "But Hong Kong belongs to Britain," he thought. "I can arrest Fogg there."

Princess Aouda, who hoped to find her cousin in Hong Kong, went too. When the ship stopped for coal in Singapore, Fogg and the princess went for a carriage ride.

They drove past pepper plants and nutmeg trees, grinning monkeys and grimacing tigers.

Near the end of the voyage, the ship battled against a raging wind. Fogg remained perfectly calm, but Passepartout was in a panic. "We'll miss our next ship, I know it!"

In the end, they reached Hong Kong one day late. Fogg had missed his next ship, which was to Yokohama in Japan.

"I knew it!" cried Passepartout.

Fix was delighted. "Now Fogg's stuck here and I can arrest him!" But luck was not on Fix's side.

It turned out that the ship to Yokohama had also been delayed, so Fogg hadn't missed it at all. Even worse, Fix's arrest papers *still* hadn't arrived.

Fix was desperate. Somehow, he had to keep Fogg in Hong Kong until the papers came.

Fogg booked a hotel for that night and set off to find Aouda's cousin. He sent Passepartout to reserve three cabins on their ship.

On the quay, Passepartout heard that the ship was sailing that very evening – and so did Fix.

"I must find my master!" the butler cried. But Fix invited him to a smoky inn for a drink first.

"I'm a detective and your master is a thief!" declared Fix, at the inn.

"Nonsense!" said Passepartout.

"Fogg mustn't know his ship sails tonight," thought Fix and bought the butler several more drinks. Before long, Passepartout was snoring and Fix had slipped away.

Fogg was on the quay early next morning and Princess Aouda was still with him. Her cousin had already left Hong Kong – and so, of course, had their ship. There was no sign of Passepartout either.

"I missed the ship too," said Fix.

The next steamer wasn't leaving for a week. But Fogg did not give up easily. Instead, he looked for another boat to take him to Japan.

Finally, Fogg found a captain of a small boat who agreed to take them to Shanghai. "You can catch another steamer for Yokohama from there," he said. Seeing Fix on the quay, Fogg offered him a lift.

Before the boat left, Fogg searched all over Hong Kong for Passepartout. But his butler had vanished.

For two days, the little boat sped through the waves. Then a great storm blew up and gigantic waves crashed upon the deck. The boat was tossed around on the sea like a ball.

When at last the wind dropped, they had lost precious time. Even with all the sails hoisted, the boat couldn't go fast enough.

Then Fogg spotted a steamer.

"That's the one from Shanghai to Yokohama," said the captain.

"Signal her," said Fogg.

With a bang, a rocket soared into the air and the ship steamed over. As soon as it reached them, Fogg, Aouda and Fix clambered aboard.

But, in the meantime, what had happened to Passepartout?

He had woken up just in time to catch the ship to Japan. Rushing on board at the last minute, he discovered – to his horror – that Fogg wasn't there.

When they landed at Yokohama, Passepartout didn't know what to do. He was wandering around in despair, when he saw a poster.

SEE THE
FAMOUS ACROBATS -
THE LONG NOSES!

LAST PERFORMANCE
BEFORE THEY LEAVE FOR
THE UNITED STATES!

"Maybe I could join the acrobats!" he said to himself. "They're going to America and that's where Fogg is heading next."

"Can you sing, standing on your head, with a top on your left foot and a sword on your right?" asked the owner of the group. Passepartout nodded. "You're in!"

That evening, he took part in his first show, at the bottom of a human triangle. The crowd loved it. But suddenly...

all the acrobats
collapsed

in a heap.

Passepartout had spotted
Phileas Fogg, jumped up and run over.

367

Chapter 5
Racing home

They had no time for explanations. Fogg and his beaming butler raced to catch their next ship, for San Francisco. Princess Aouda, who had nowhere else to go, came too. She grew fonder of Fogg each day.

As the ship steamed on, Passepartout began to think Fogg would win his bet. But one day he saw Fix on deck. The inspector had secretly followed them.

Passepartout hit him.

"Wait!" cried Fix. "It might have seemed I was against you before..."

"You were!" said Passepartout.

"Well, yes," agreed Fix, "and I still think Fogg's a thief. But now I want him in England. It's only in England I can arrest him."

Passepartout didn't want to worry Fogg, so he kept quiet about Fix. But when Fogg went to get his passport stamped in San Francisco, he bumped into the inspector too.

"What a surprise!" lied Fix and joined them on the next stage of the journey, crossing America by train.

The Pacific Railroad steamed right across the country to New York. It had every luxury on board, from shops to restaurants, but it still had to wait when a herd of buffalo crossed the track.

370

The next obstacle was a shaky bridge. "I'll cross at top speed!" said the driver. He went so fast the wheels barely touched the tracks.

The train reared up and jumped across. As it landed on the other side, the bridge crashed into the river.

Soon after that, they hit real trouble. The train was steaming by some rocky cliffs, when a band of Sioux warriors jumped onto its roof. The warriors quickly took over driving the train. "There is a fort near the next station," shouted a guard. "If only we could stop the train."

Passepartout sped into action.

Crawling under the train, he wriggled and swung all the way to the engine, without being seen.

Then, he unhooked the engine and the train slowly came to a halt... just beside the station.

But when Fogg looked for his butler a few seconds later, he'd gone.

"The warriors took him when they fled!" shouted a guard.

Calling over some soldiers, Fogg went into the hills to look for him.

It took all day to find and free Passepartout. They had to camp out overnight and only got back to the station the following morning.

By then, their train had long since left and the next one wasn't due until that evening.

"I've done it again," wailed the butler. But Fix came to the rescue.

"I've just met a man who owns a land yacht," he announced.

Soon, they were gliding over the snow. Wind filled the yacht's sails and it whizzed over the icy plains.

They caught up with the train for New York at the very next station. It puffed across the country at top speed. Fogg still had a chance.

They finally stopped at a station by the steamship pier, on the bank of the River Hudson in New York. But the ship to England had already left — it had sailed just forty-five minutes earlier.

No other steamers could take them across the Atlantic Ocean in time. Passepartout was crushed, but Fogg visited every ship in the port. Once again, he found a captain who would take passengers.

The ship was sailing to France, but that didn't worry Fogg. He simply locked the captain in his cabin and changed course.

The ship was fast, but it was now winter and the weather was terrible. Then the engineer gave Fogg more bad news.

"The coal for the boiler is running out!" he said grimly.

"Even my clever master can't solve this," thought Passepartout.

Once again, Fogg surprised him. He ordered the sailors to cut down the mast and chop it into logs.

Then he told the astonished men to burn the wood in the ship's boiler.

Over the next three days, the sailors burned the ship's bridge...

the cabins...

and even the decks.

By the time they reached England, only the ship's metal hull was left.

They landed in Liverpool, with just enough time for Fogg to catch a train to London and win his bet. But, as Fogg stepped off the ship, Fix made his move.

"Phileas Fogg," the detective announced, "I arrest you for stealing fifty-five thousand pounds."

Fogg was thrown into prison and there
was absolutely nothing Princess Aouda or
Passepartout could do.

Three hours later, they were waiting for news,
when Fix rushed in. His hair was a mess and he
looked ashamed.

"I've made a dreadful mistake," he cried. "The
real thief was arrested three days ago!"

Fogg was free again. But he had only five and
a half hours left.

Fogg, calm as ever, paid for a special train which roared down to London. As it pulled in, he checked the station clock – 8:55. Fogg had lost his bet by just ten minutes.

"I can't believe it," Passepartout cried.

"We came so close."

Chapter 6
What next?

Phileas Fogg did not show any sign of how
he felt. He simply left the station with
Passepartout and Aouda and drove home. The
next day, he stayed in his room, adding up all
the money he had lost.

At seven o'clock, Fogg visited Princess Aouda in her room.

"Madam," he said sadly, "When I brought you to England, I planned to give you a fortune. But I am afraid now it is not possible."

"My dear sir," the princess replied gently, "I don't want your money... just you."

"You want to marry me?" He couldn't believe what he was hearing.

Fogg was overjoyed and, for the first time in his life, it showed. "Passepartout!" he called. "Run to the church and book our wedding for tomorrow!"

"On a Monday?" Passepartout asked.

"On a Monday," Fogg laughed.

Meanwhile Fogg's friends at his club had spent the last few days in a fever of excitement. They had not heard a word from Fogg since he left on October 2nd.

On the evening of December 21st, they waited eagerly to see if he would show. And, as the hands on the clock reached 8:44, they heard a knock on the door.

386

It was Phileas Fogg in person. But how had he done it? Well, Passepartout had returned from the priest with incredible news.

"Not Monday tomorrow," he gasped. "Tomorrow, Sunday. Today is… SATURDAY!"

Going around the world to the east had gained Fogg an extra day. He'd had ten minutes left to get to the club and win his bet.

Fogg won twenty thousand pounds but, as he had spent nearly nineteen thousand pounds on the way, he wasn't much better off.

On the other hand, he did find a wife and happiness on his trip. Most people would go around the world for less!

Fogg's route

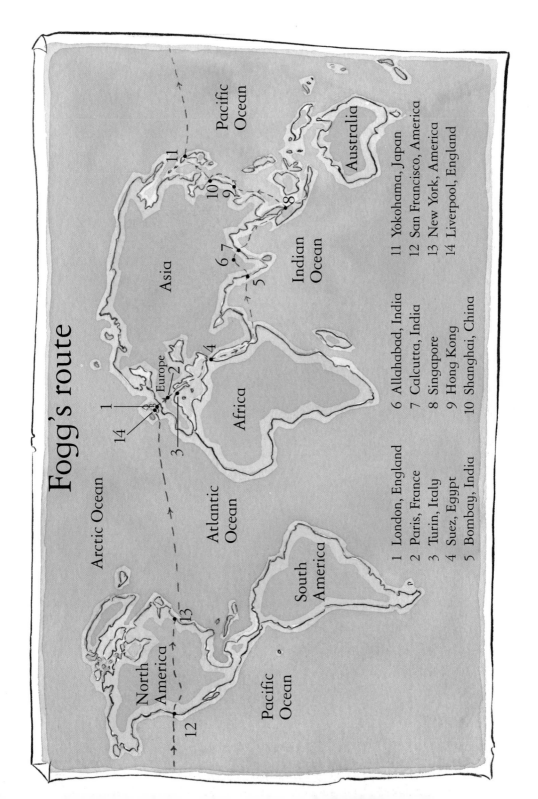

Arctic Ocean

Pacific Ocean

Asia

Europe

Africa

Australia

Indian Ocean

Atlantic Ocean

North America

South America

Pacific Ocean

1 London, England
2 Paris, France
3 Turin, Italy
4 Suez, Egypt
5 Bombay, India

6 Allahabad, India
7 Calcutta, India
8 Singapore
9 Hong Kong
10 Shanghai, China

11 Yokohama, Japan
12 San Francisco, America
13 New York, America
14 Liverpool, England

Heidi

Johanna Spyri (1827-1901)

Johanna Spyri, a doctor's daughter, was born in the Swiss countryside and grew up loving the mountains. Her first book, *A Leaf on Vrony's Grave*, was published in 1871, and was followed by many stories for both adults and children. *Heidi* was published nine years later. It was an instant success, and remains as popular as ever today.

Chapter 1
Meeting Grandfather

Heidi felt cross and tired as Aunt Dete pulled her up the steep slope.

"I'd go faster if I wasn't wearing *all* my clothes," said Heidi.

"You'll need them at your grandfather's and I don't want to carry them," said her aunt, angrily.

"Do you think Grandfather will want me?" Heidi asked nervously.

Aunt Dete shook her head. "I don't know. He's a miserable old man and he hasn't seen you since you were a baby. But I've taken care of you for long enough. Now it's his turn."

At last they reached
Grandfather's hut, at the
very top of the mountain.
Dete rapped sharply on
the door. It creaked
open and an old
man peered out.

"What do you want?"
he asked, gruffly.

395

"This is your granddaughter, Heidi," Dete explained. "Your dead son's child. I've brought her to live with you."

"Take her away," said the old man, trying to shut the door. "I don't want her."

"I don't care," Dete snapped. "You have to take her. Both her parents are dead. I've found a good job in Frankfurt and she can't come with me."

With that,
Heidi's aunt turned
and ran down the mountain.

397

Grandfather stared silently at Heidi.
Heidi stared back.

"He doesn't want me," she thought, sadly,
"but where else can I go?"

"Well... you'd better come in," said
Grandfather, with a scowl.

Heidi stepped into the hut and looked around. There didn't seem to be room for her anywhere.

"Where shall I sleep?" she asked. Grandfather shrugged. He didn't even look at her. "You'll have to find your own bed," he growled.

399

Heidi looked again and saw a ladder in the corner. Feeling curious, she climbed up into a hayloft. From the window, she could see a green valley far below and hear pine trees whooshing in the wind.

She lifted some of the sweet-smelling hay, puffing it up into the shape of a mattress. "I'll sleep here," she called. "It's lovely!"

"She shows some sense," Grandfather muttered to himself. "Come down now," he ordered. "It's time for supper."

Heidi watched Grandfather blow onto the embers of the fire, making the flames blaze. Bringing a bowl, he filled it to the brim with rich, creamy milk.

"Here you are," he said. Then he toasted bread and cheese over the fire until they were a glorious golden brown.

Delicious smells filled the hut and Heidi realized how hungry she was. She licked up oozing drips of cheese, crunched the toast and drank the milk to the last drop.

Through the open door, she saw the sky and mountainside glow in the setting sun. "I like it here, Grandfather," she said.

That night, Heidi snuggled down in the hayloft.
As she fell asleep she wondered why Grandfather
lived all alone, high on the mountain. What had
happened to make him so sad and unfriendly?

Chapter 2
The goat boy

Early next morning, Heidi woke to the sound of bells. She sat up. Sunshine poured through the hayloft window, turning her straw bed into shimmering gold.

Quickly, she dressed and shot down the ladder.
A boy was standing at the door, whistling.

"This is Peter, the goat boy," Grandfather told
her. "He's come for Little Swan and Little Bear."

Two goats – one white, one brown – pushed
past him and sniffed Heidi. She giggled as they
licked her hands.

"Their tongues tickle!" she said.

"Do you want to come with me?" Peter
shouted over the bleats and bells. "I'm going up
the mountain to find fresh grass for them."

"Can I?" Heidi asked Grandfather.

"I suppose," he replied. "But have your
breakfast first." He sat on a stool and milked
Little Bear, then handed Heidi a bowl of
fresh milk.

"Come on!" said Peter, as soon as she'd finished. "You can stay at the back and make sure none of the goats get lost."

As they ran over rocks to the mountain pastures, Peter showed Heidi all the mountain's secrets.

He pointed to an eagle's nest hidden in the craggy peaks and the spots where wild flowers grew. The mountain looked as if a giant had scattered handfuls of jewels over it.

Heidi had never seen so many flowers. She picked great blue and yellow bunches for Grandfather.

409

Every day, Heidi went out with Peter and the goats. And every day, her cheeks grew rosier and her eyes more sparkly. Grandfather fed her crusty bread, tasty cheese and Little Swan's milk. At night, he told her stories by the fire.

Heidi had never been happier... until one morning, when the door flew open and there stood Aunt Dete in a brand new dress.

"I've come for Heidi," she announced. "I should never have left her with you in the first place."

"No," cried Heidi, suddenly afraid. "I like it here. I want to stay with Grandfather."

Dete ignored her. "I've found a place for Heidi in Frankfurt," she told Grandfather. "Clara Sesemann, a little girl who's always ill, wants a friend to keep her company."

"If Heidi behaves," her aunt went on, "Mr. Sesemann will pay her and buy her some fine new clothes. It's a great chance for her."

Grandfather had been looking crosser and crosser during this speech. "Take her and spoil her then!" he bellowed at Dete. "But don't bother coming back. Ever!"

Ignoring Heidi's protests, Dete gripped her arm and dragged her outside. As they left, Heidi saw Grandfather sitting alone, his head in his hands.

"Poor Grandfather!" cried Heidi, tears trickling down her face.

"Come *on*, Heidi," said Dete, pushing her down the mountain. "I'm sorry I ever left you with that sad old man."

"Why is he so sad?" asked Heidi.

"He thinks the world is a bad place," her aunt replied. "First, his wife died. Then your father, his only child, wasted all his money and died too. But your grandfather's just made things worse for himself."

"He said there was only misery in the world and shut himself away up here. Forget him, Heidi. Think about Frankfurt."

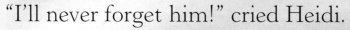

"I'll never forget him!" cried Heidi.

"It's for your own good," Dete declared, striding off.

Heidi was quiet, but secretly she made a promise. "One day I'll come back to him."

Chapter 3
Heidi and Clara

It was a long journey to Frankfurt. The sun was beginning to set when they stopped before a grand house in a cobbled street.

Dete pulled the bell. "This is it," she muttered.

A well-dressed servant opened the door and led them into a vast hall.

Heidi felt very small and shabby. She felt even worse when the housekeeper, Mrs. Rotenmeyer, saw her.

"You look most unsuitable," she said to Heidi with a sigh. "I suppose you'd better meet Clara."

Clara lay on a heap of pillows in a frilly four-poster bed. Her face was pale and the room was hot.

"Thank you for coming, Heidi," she said, quietly. "I'll like having company. I can't get out of bed."

"Why not?" asked Heidi.

"I've been sick and I'm still weak," Clara explained. "I don't think I'll ever get better."

"No one could get better in this hot, stuffy room," Heidi thought. She ran over to a window and flung it wide open.

The street below jostled with people, horses and carriages. Heidi could hear strange music mixed in with the clattering hooves and footsteps.

Leaning out, she saw a ragged boy with a street organ. A pair of kittens peeked out of his pockets.

Heidi rushed downstairs and onto the street. "Can you come here?" she called, beckoning him over. "There's someone I want you to play for."

Moments later, they were both bounding up the stairs.

"Surprise!" shouted Heidi, throwing open Clara's door and letting in the ragged boy.

Downstairs, Mrs. Rotenmeyer the housekeeper was puzzled. She could hear singing, laughing, music, even kittens – and all coming from Clara's bedroom.

"What's going on in here?" she shrieked, as she stormed into Clara's room.

"How did this dreadful boy get in?" she demanded. "I blame you," she said, glaring at Heidi. "I knew you were trouble from the moment I saw you. Go to your room at once."

"No," pleaded Clara. "Heidi was only trying to cheer me up." She held Heidi's hand. "Please don't send Heidi to her room. We want to have our supper together."

There was nothing Mrs. Rotenmeyer could do. She had to obey Clara. "All right," she said crossly, turning to go, "but get that dirty boy out of here now!"

Mrs. Rotenmeyer returned carrying a tray loaded with rich food. Greasy chunks of meat swam in a cream sauce. Clara pushed it around her plate and hardly ate anything. Heidi didn't like it either.

"I don't get hungry lying in bed," Clara murmured.

"You'd soon get hungry running up the mountain to Grandfather's hut," Heidi told her.

Clara looked sad. "But since I've been ill, I can't walk."

"That's terrible," said Heidi.

The warm room and heavy meal were making her feel sleepy. She had to go outside to breathe some fresh air.

Stale smells hung over the noisy, dirty, street. Heidi longed for the cool clear air of the mountain and the soft breeze that made the pine trees rustle.

Some time after Heidi's arrival, the servants started claiming the house was haunted by a ghost.

"A white figure floats down the stairs at night," said a maid.

The servants were so upset, Mrs. Rotenmeyer grew worried. "I must tell Clara's father," she decided.

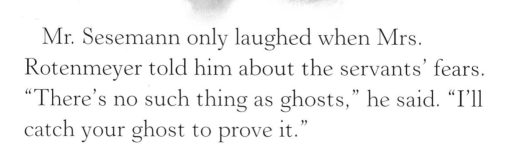

Mr. Sesemann only laughed when Mrs. Rotenmeyer told him about the servants' fears. "There's no such thing as ghosts," he said. "I'll catch your ghost to prove it."

The next night he waited in the hall
at the bottom of the stairs. Heidi came
down, wearing a white nightgown. She
tried to open the locked front door,
then sobbed.

Mr. Sesemann went over to her and saw she
was still fast asleep.

"Heidi has been sleepwalking," Mr. Sesemann explained to Clara and Mrs. Rotenmeyer, the next morning. "The poor child is so homesick, I think she'd better go home."

Clara looked sad. "I'll miss you, Heidi," she said.

Chapter 4
Heidi goes home

The following week, Grandfather looked out of the window and could hardly believe his eyes. A peculiar procession was stumbling up the mountain slope.

429

Two men were struggling with suitcases. A
third hauled a wheelchair and a fourth carried
a child bundled up in a shawl. The men puffed
and panted, their shirts drenched in sweat.

Ahead of them all danced Heidi.

She raced up the slope and threw herself into Grandfather's arms.

"Heidi!" he cried. "You've come back to me. I thought I'd never see you again."

"I missed you," Heidi said. "Look, Mr. Sesemann has written you a letter to explain."

Dear Sir,

Heidi was too homesick to stay with us but Clara could not bear to say goodbye. I hope you will forgive me for sending her with Heidi to stay for a month.

Clara, alas, is still very weak after a long illness. She has no appetite and cannot walk. I hope her visit to you on the mountain will give her new strength.

With all my thanks and best wishes,

Yours sincerely,

Hans Sesemann

Grandfather turned to Clara.

"I'm very pleased to meet you," he said. "And thank you for bringing Heidi back to me. You'll soon feel better breathing our mountain air."

Grandfather put Clara's wheelchair in the sunshine, so she could see the wonderful view, and gave her a bowl of fresh milk.

"Guess who really gave you the milk?" Heidi teased, bringing Little Swan over. The goat butted Clara gently, until she realized Little Swan wanted to be stroked.

Clara drank thirstily. "This tastes much nicer than Frankfurt milk," she said.

"Heidi?" came a shout. Peter ran up the path to them. "I heard you were back," he said to Heidi.

"Come out with me tomorrow," he urged her.

"Peter, I can't," said Heidi. "I have to stay with Clara."

Peter gave Clara a jealous look.

"You go Heidi," Clara insisted. "I'll be fine."

All the same, when they set off next morning, Clara looked sad.

"I'll be quick," Heidi promised. "I just want to climb the ridge where the biggest, bluest flowers grow."

Clara watched them go longingly. She would have given anything to be running with them, with strong legs that could skip and jump.

"I wish you'd come," Heidi told Clara when she returned. "We watched an eagle soar above our heads and did somersaults down the mountain."

Clara sighed. "Oh I wish I could walk!"

"Cheer up," said Grandfather. "The sun has already brought roses to your cheeks. I'm sure you'll soon feel stronger."

"And I won't leave you again," Heidi promised.

From where he stood, high on the mountain, Peter could see Heidi and Clara talking together. His heart burned with jealousy.

"I wish that girl hadn't come," he thought. "Heidi's *my* friend. I'll *make* Clara go home." And a plan began to form in his mind.

Chapter 5
Peter's plan

Before sunrise next morning, Peter crept to Grandfather's hut. All was quiet and still.

Just as Peter hoped, Clara's wheelchair stood by the door. Noiselessly, he pushed it to the edge of the mountain and rolled it over a steep, stony cliff.

The chair hit the rocks with a terrible clatter. An endless echo followed its fall, BANG... CLANG... again and again.

Peering over the cliff, Peter saw the jagged rocks had smashed the wheelchair into a thousand pieces. Peter looked at what he had done... and fled.

439

When he arrived at the hut for the
goats, Heidi told Peter about
Clara's chair. "The wind must
have caught it," she said.

"Grandfather has to carry Clara everywhere."

"Then Clara will have to go home, won't she?"
Peter demanded.

"Aha," murmured Grandfather. "I think I
know who blew that puff of wind."

Heidi was shocked. "Did you do it, Peter?" she asked, sharply.

Peter went red. "I'm... I'm sorry," he stammered. "I wanted her to go. You don't have time for me now."

"Peter, you must hate me," said Clara. "You think I've taken Heidi away from you."

"Never mind," Heidi interrupted. "We can all still be friends."

But Grandfather shook his head.

"Mr. Sesemann may not be so forgiving," he said. "Clara's chair is still broken."

"If only Clara could walk..." said Heidi.
"I do feel stronger," Clara whispered.
"Perhaps I could try."

She edged herself forward and put her slender feet on the ground. Grandfather gently took hold of her hands and helped her to stand.

"My legs feel so weak," said Clara, trembling.

"Be brave," said Grandfather.

Slowly, Clara put one foot in front of the other.

Clara wobbled, but Grandfather supported
her.

"Rest now," he ordered. "You can try
again tomorrow."

Every day, Clara walked a little more. Hungry
from the exercise and fresh mountain air, she
wolfed down huge meals. Strength flowed into
her and she tingled with energy. "Won't Father
be amazed?" she thought.

Chapter 6
A surprise for Mr. Sesemann

A few weeks later, Mr. Sesemann arrived for Clara. He hardly recognized his daughter with her glowing face, bright eyes and thick, shiny hair.

445

When Clara stood up, he was astonished and when she walked up to him, he had to sit down. "Is it really you?" he said. "I can't believe it. You're walking!"

"Isn't it wonderful," laughed Clara. "Grandfather and Heidi made it happen."

"And Peter," Grandfather put in, his eyes twinkling.

"You did it, Clara," said Heidi. "It was your hard work."

"It's a miracle," Mr. Sesemann beamed. "Clara, I'm proud of you. Thank you, thank you everyone."

"You must come back to the mountain whenever you want," Heidi told Clara.

"And you must come to Frankfurt – Peter too," said Clara. "We'll find the ragged boy again and dance."

When Clara and her father had gone, Heidi and Grandfather went outside to watch the sunset. The sky and mountains shone red-gold, just like Heidi's first evening.

"It's beautiful," said Grandfather.

"Once I was sad and lonely," he told Heidi, "but you've made me a happy man."

Moonfleet

John Meade Falkner (1858-1932)

John Meade Falkner was born in Wiltshire, England. He wrote *Moonfleet*, an action-filled tale of smuggling, in 1898, basing Moonfleet village on East Fleet, a fishing village on the English south coast. The story is set in the mid-18th century, when smugglers lurked around the south coast of England. These were men who hid goods brought from other countries, so they didn't have to pay taxes on them. Government officials, known as magistrates, did everything they could to stop the smugglers – even if that meant killing them.

Chapter 1
Moonfleet village

My name is John Trenchard, and I was fifteen years old when this story began, on a stormy night in Moonfleet village.

Fierce winds swept from the sea, shaking our houses, shattering windows, and sending tiles flying from roofs. In the bay, huge waves broke over the cliffs, flooding the cobbled streets.

The next morning, we had to tiptoe through mud as the church bells called us to the Sunday service. We all sat wrapped up in thick coats as Mr. Glennie, the minister, began his sermon. Suddenly, a strange noise echoed around the walls – a knocking sound, like boats jostling at sea. Everyone jumped up, listening to the eerie noises. They were coming from the vault under the church.

"It's Blackbeard!" someone shouted. Everyone shuddered. Blackbeard was the nickname of John Mohune, a rich noble who owned the village over a hundred years ago. His tomb sat beneath the church, but many villagers believed his ghost still haunted Moonfleet, protecting treasure he had buried before he died.

Mr. Glennie just laughed. "The noises aren't ghosts," he said. "The floods have filled the vault with water, and the sounds are coffins banging against each other as they float."

Still, I wasn't convinced. The coffins in the vault were a hundred years old, and would surely be rotten by now. The noises we'd heard sounded like solid wood.

After the service I crept outside to investigate. Usually, the heavy stone entrance to the vault was sealed shut, but the floods had forced it open. To my amazement, I could see a dark tunnel leading under the church.

All I could think about was Blackbeard's treasure. Could it be hidden inside his vault? I was desperate to find out. But I would have to go home for a candle and, anyway, I was late for lunch. I decided to return later to hunt for the treasure.

Chapter 2
The secret vault

Back home, Aunt Jane greeted me with a scowl. "You're late John," she snapped. "Your lunch is cold now."

My parents had died when I was very young, and I had lived with my aunt ever since. She was a stern woman, who rarely allowed me out of the house. So, that night, I waited until I heard her snoring in her room, then grabbed a candle and slipped out in secret.

457

I was so excited about the treasure, I didn't even feel scared until I reached the churchyard. Then I remembered the noises from beneath the church, and the stories of Blackbeard's ghost. But the lure of treasure drew me on, and soon I was back at the entrance to Blackbeard's vault.

I lit the candle and stepped inside. My heart was pounding as I followed a tunnel to a set of steps that curved under the church. At the bottom lay a dark chamber.

Inside, several old coffins lay on shelves around the walls. But the floor of the vault was filled with brand new barrels. To my horror, I realized I had discovered a smugglers' hideout. It must have been these barrels that had made the noises we heard in church.

I had to get out – smugglers were dangerous men, who didn't look kindly on spying eyes. But, as I turned to go, I heard a voice in the tunnel. Someone was coming!

459

I quickly snuffed out my candle, and hid
behind a coffin as two men entered the vault
and set down some more barrels. Peeking over
the edge, I saw that one of them was the church
groundskeeper, Ratsey, and the other was Elzivir
Block, who owned a local inn called the *Why
Not*. Last year, his son David had been shot and
killed by Maskew, a local magistrate who had
caught him smuggling.

Eventually, the smugglers left and I climbed from my hiding place. Dizzy from the stale vault air, I slipped and knocked the lid from a coffin. Inside, a body lay wrapped in cloth. Part of it was torn, and I could see bushy black hair around the figure's neck. I was sure it was Blackbeard. Could his treasure be inside the coffin?

With trembling hands, I relit the candle. A silver locket hung around Blackbeard's neck. I lifted it away, hoping to find some jewels inside, but all it held was a scrap of paper with what seemed to be a prayer written on it.

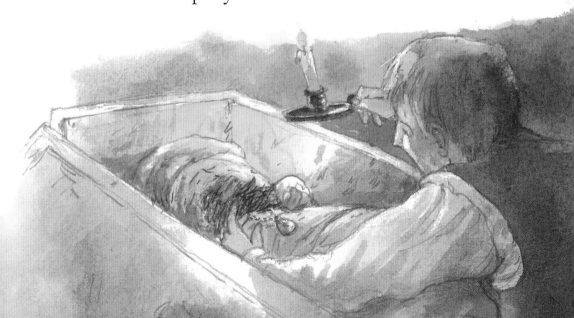

Disappointed, I looped the locket around my neck and returned along the tunnel. But now I discovered the entrance had been sealed. The smugglers must have covered it when they left. I pushed at the stone blocking my way out, but I couldn't shift it.

Now I realized why I had felt dizzy – there was no air here underground. Crazy with panic, I bashed at the door, screaming for help. But it was no good. My candle burned out. Everything went dark and I fell to the floor.

Chapter 3
Elzivir Block

I woke to find myself lying in bed. At first I thought that everything had been a dream, but then I felt the locket around my neck and knew I had been rescued.

The door creaked open, and Elzivir Block came in. I thought he would be furious that I had found his smugglers' den, but instead he smiled and handed me a bowl of soup. As I drank it, he told me how he and Ratsey had heard my shouts from the vault. They had raced back and found me lying unconscious inside. I was now upstairs in Elzivir's inn, the *Why Not*.

"You can stay here until you're well again," Elzivir said.

I stayed in bed for several days. All the time, Elzivir looked after me like a nurse. I had always thought he was stern and fierce, but I have never known anyone kinder than he was then.

Elzivir had already told my aunt where I was, but when I finally returned to her house, she refused to let me in. "You chose to run away," she snapped, "so now you can stay away."

I was homeless. The only friend I had was Elzivir, so I returned to the *Why Not* and told him what had happened.

"You must live here then," he said. "There's plenty of room."

So, I began to live with Elzivir at the old tavern. In the mornings I went to school, but I spent my afternoons helping him in the gardens or with his boats in the bay. Elzivir had lived alone since his son died, and I think he was glad for the company. He rarely mentioned David, but spoke often about his hatred for Mr. Maskew, the magistrate who killed him.

One afternoon, I was walking in the woods when I met Maskew's daughter, Grace. I knew Grace Maskew from school. She was pretty and kind and I had always liked her. As we walked together, I couldn't help telling her everything that had happened. Grace looked worried.

"John," she said, "please be careful."

I knew what Grace meant. Elzivir was a smuggler, and now that I was living with him, she thought I might become one myself. Grace's father hated smugglers, and was determined to rid Moonfleet of them all. One evening, I discovered just how determined he was.

Elzivir and I were playing cards
in the *Why Not*, when the magistrate
burst through the door. Elzivir leapt up, his
face red with rage. "You're not welcome in my
house," he cried.

"Your house?" Maskew said, "Not for long!" and he threw a piece of paper onto the bar.

Elzivir read it in silence, then handed it to me. It was about the *Why Not*. He had never owned the tavern, but rented it from a local landlord. Now Maskew had offered the landlord more money than Elzivir to buy it for himself.

"I want you both out by next week," he said, slamming the door as he left.

"Elzivir," I cried, "what will we do? We don't have enough money to keep the *Why Not*."

"There is one way," Elzivir replied. "A smugglers' ship is bringing a new cargo into Hoar Head Bay tomorrow night. It's a heavy load, and the job will pay well for the men who help carry it ashore. Will you join us?"

Smuggling! The thought terrified me, but Elzivir had been so kind, I was determined not to let him down. "I will," I said.

That night, I met Grace in the woods, and
told her the news. She was still worried about
the danger of smuggling, and scared I might
get caught.

"It's only once," I promised her, "and when
I return, I'll have made my own money."

"Then I'll keep a candle burning in my
window until you do," she said.

Chapter 4
Hoar Head Bay

It was midnight when Elzivir and I
reached Hoar Head Bay. Several other
smugglers were already on the beach,
hiding in the shadows by the cliff. Seeing
that I was with Elzivir, they greeted me as
a friend.

"The ship should arrive soon," they told me.
"Wait with us."

Several hours passed. I sat beside some rocks,
at first fidgeting with nerves.

At last, there came a shout. "The ship,"
someone yelled. "It's here!"

470

Everyone rushed to pull the ship up onto the pebbly beach. Heavy barrels, filled with brandy, were passed down from the deck and packed into carts. Soon they were all unloaded, and the ship was heading back out to sea. Just then, one of the smugglers spotted a figure hiding among some rocks. "Over there," he cried. "A spy!"

Several of the smugglers chased off after the figure. A few minutes later, they returned dragging a prisoner – Mr. Maskew!

"Shoot him," someone said.

"Don't touch him," Elzivir shouted. "Leave him with me, and go your ways."

Everyone knew that Maskew had killed Elzivir's son. Now was his chance for revenge. Taking the barrels, the other smugglers left us alone with our prisoner.

Elzivir raised a pistol to the magistrate's head. His hand shook with rage.

"Spare me, Mr. Block," Maskew grovelled. "Oh, spare me please!"

"Elzivir," I pleaded. "Don't shoot!" I hated Maskew too, but I couldn't let Elzivir kill him – he was Grace's father.

Elzivir looked at me, and I saw his pistol lower. Then a shout came from above.

"Stop! In the name of the King!" Dozens of soldiers appeared at the top of the cliff.

"Over here," Maskew yelled. "Save me!"

The soldiers raised their rifles and fired. Elzivir and I dived away, but the bullets tore into Mr. Maskew, killing him instantly.

"Run for the cliffs," Elzivir shouted.

I began to run, but the soldiers fired again and a bullet hit my leg. Elzivir rushed over and lifted me up. The pain was incredible.

"I'm sorry, John," he said, "but the soldiers will think we killed Maskew. If they catch us, we will hang for sure."

473

The only escape was a narrow path that zig-zagged up the steep side of a cliff. Below us was a huge drop, but Elzivir never slipped and never let me fall. When we reached the top, I lay on the soft grass, gasping with pain.

"We must keep moving, lad," Elzivir said. "Those soldiers will find a way up soon enough."

Elzivir lifted me onto his back and we continued, crossing fields and streams, until we reached an old stone quarry and the entrance to a cave.

Elzivir gave me some water to drink and made
a fire. "We can hide here until your leg is healed,"
he said. "Then we must find passage overseas on
a smuggling ship."

Several weeks passed as I recovered. Elzivir
cleaned the wound each day and talked to
me to keep my mind off the pain. He had to
risk leaving the cave to find us food, and was
sometimes gone for several days at a time.

Alone at night, the cave terrified me. The wind
screamed through the entrance, and the fire cast
eerie shadows around the walls. I sat clutching
the locket I had stolen from Blackbeard's coffin,
and read the prayer written inside. I hoped it
would guard me against evil spirits.

Then, one night, I noticed something strange about the writing. Four of the words were written in darker ink than the others.

*From eight to **eighty** I shall trek*
*Until my **feet** are tired and worn*
*But as I walk **down** life's hard road*
*God's love will keep me **well** and warm*

As I stared at the words, my thoughts returned to Blackbeard's treasure. Was this a code to reveal its hiding place? When I showed Elzivir, his eyes lit up.

"John," he said, "before Blackbeard came to Moonfleet, he lived in Carisbrook Castle. The castle is a prison now, but I have heard that there is a deep well inside!"

"Elzivir," I cried, "the treasure must be hidden in that well – eighty feet down."

Chapter 5
The well

Dark clouds rumbled over Carisbrook Castle as we approached. Elzivir rang a bell beside the huge iron gate. Moments later, it creaked open and the prison guard grinned at us with dirty brown teeth. We had met him in secret the night before, and he'd agreed to take us to the prison's well in exchange for a share of the treasure. He had a shifty look about him that I didn't trust, but we had no choice. "Come on," he snarled. "Hurry up!"

We followed him along a dark corridor, and I heard prisoners moaning inside their cells. The guard unlocked one of the old doors and heaved it open. Inside, a barred window let in enough light to see a dark hole in the floor, with a dirty bucket hanging above it on a rope. I peered into the grimy pit, remembering Blackbeard's message – eighty feet down. Below, the murky darkness seemed to go on forever.

"There's the well," the guard said. "Now, where's this treasure?"

"We think it's in this well," I said. "I'm the lightest, so why don't you both lower me down in the bucket? If you stop when you've let out eighty feet of rope, I should be in the right place."

"John," Elzivir whispered, "be careful. I have already lost my son. I would rather lose all the treasure in the world than lose you too."

I climbed into the bucket, and Elzivir and the
guard lowered me into the dreadful depths.
Above, the hole grew smaller and smaller.

"John," Elzivir shouted finally, "you're eighty
feet deep now."

Raising the guard's lamp, I looked around.
The bricks were mossy and worn with age.
But I noticed that one of them was not as
old as the others. My heart raced – had I found
it? I carefully pulled the brick from the wall.
Behind it was a small gap... and in it sat a tiny
bag. My fingers trembled as I pulled it out and
peered inside.

"Have you found anything?"
the guard shouted.

Inside the bag was a huge
diamond, the size of a walnut.

"Yes," I shouted, "I've
found the treasure!
Pull me up!"

As soon as I reached the top, I jumped from the bucket, holding up the bag triumphantly. Then I froze – the guard was pointing a pistol right at me.

"Give me the treasure," he growled, "or I'll kill you."

Suddenly, Elzivir leapt at him and they fell into a savage fight. The guard was bigger than Elzivir, but not as strong. Just as he charged again, Elzivir flipped him over his shoulder. I heard a terrible scream as the guard plunged into the well and fell to his death.

"Quickly John," Elzivir cried, "another guard might come."

The prison gates slammed shut behind us as we raced away with the treasure.

Chapter 6
The diamond dealer

That night, Elzivir arranged for a ship to take us to The Hague, a city in Holland. He had heard that it was a good place to sell jewels. I sat on deck, holding the diamond and watching it sparkle in the moonlight. Elzivir stared at the stone too, but he looked worried.

484

"John," he said, "ever since you first looked for that treasure, luck has run against you. I think that diamond is cursed."

But I didn't listen. Instead, I thought about how I would return to Moonfleet a rich man and marry Grace.

In The Hague, we learned that the richest diamond dealer, a man named Mr. Aldobrand, lived in a huge white mansion on the outskirts of the town. I knocked on the door, and an old man with wrinkled skin answered.

"Are you Mr. Aldobrand?" I asked. "We've come all the way from Moonfleet with a diamond to sell."

The old man plucked the jewel from my hand, and studied it for a long moment.

"Come in then," he said finally.

Mr. Aldobrand led us along a hallway, where several guards sat watching us suspiciously.

"Don't worry about them," Mr. Aldobrand muttered, "they're just for security."

He guided us into a study filled with dusty books. The sun was just setting and its red light fell through the large bay windows. Mr. Aldobrand sat at a desk inspecting the diamond with a magnifying glass as I fidgeted with suspense.

"Well," I asked, "how much is it worth?"

"Nothing," Mr. Aldobrand said. "I am sorry, but this diamond is a fake. It's glass."

"Fake?" I said. "That's not possible!"

"I assure you it is," he replied. "But I will still pay you ten pounds for it."

Elzivir snatched the jewel from the desk. "We did not come here for pennies," he cried. "I am glad to be rid of the thing!" And he hurled the diamond out of the window.

I watched in horror as the jewel landed in a flowerbed outside. Elzivir stormed off, but as I went to follow him, I caught Mr. Aldobrand looking to see where the diamond landed too.

Outside, I told Elzivir what I had seen.

"I don't think the diamond is fake at all," I said. "Mr. Aldobrand was lying to buy it cheaply. We have to find it before he does."

Elzivir gripped my shoulders and looked me in the eye. I had never seen him so serious. "John," he said, "that diamond is cursed. Let it be."

How desperately I wish that I had listened to him, but instead I crept off down the side of the house, and climbed a wall into Mr. Aldobrand's garden.

Elzivir followed in silence.

It was darker now, though there was still enough moonlight to look for the diamond. But when I reached the flowerbed where it had landed, the jewel was gone.

"Elzivir," I whispered. "Mr. Aldobrand has already taken it."

"Then let us go home," Elzivir pleaded.

"No," I said. "He must have it inside the house."

Before Elzivir could stop me, I ran to the back of the house and peeked through a gap in the curtains. Inside, Mr. Aldobrand sat at his desk. He had a self-satisfied grin on his face... and our diamond in his hand.

Rage built up inside me. I hurled myself
forward, smashing through the window and into
the study.

"Thieves!" Mr. Aldobrand screeched. "Help!"

I grabbed the diamond from him, but the
door crashed open and Aldobrand's guards
charged in carrying clubs. Three of them
attacked Elzivir, and two came for me, raining
blows on us with sticks and fists. The last thing
I saw was the diamond falling to the floor, and
then I did the same.

Chapter 7
Prisoners

Elzivir and I were thrown into a cold prison cell and left in the dark. I slumped in a corner, aching from the blows from the guards' clubs.

Several days later, the door burst open and guards marched us to a courthouse. There, Mr. Aldobrand told the judge that we had broken into his house to steal his diamond.

"Liar!" I shouted, but a guard struck me on the head.

"You are both greedy thieves," the judge said, "and I sentence you to work on a chain gang – for the rest of your lives."

As the guards led us away, I leaned over to Mr. Aldobrand. "Now you have the treasure," I told him, "and may it curse you the way it has me."

Elzivir and I were shackled in irons and marched with hundreds of other criminals to a place called Ymeguen, where we were made to build a new fortress. Guards stood by with whips and guns as we toiled in the blistering summer sun.

Elzivir was put to work on a different part of the building, so I barely saw him any more. Instead, I worked alone, thinking about the pain I had caused him, and how much I missed Grace back in Moonfleet.

Ten years later, when I was 26, the fortress was finally finished. One morning, the guards handed some of us over to soldiers, who led us onto a ship at a nearby dock. "Please, where are we going?" I begged one of them.

"Java," he laughed, and lashed me with his whip.

My heart broke. Java was a slave colony on the other side of the world. No prisoner who went there ever returned.

The guards shoved us onto the ship and into a tiny room below deck. Another group of prisoners was already down there, crammed in like pigs in a pen. As my eyes adjusted to the dark, I thought I saw a familiar face. It was Elzivir! His hair was turning white, and his body looked old and tired, but he still found a smile for me.

"I am sorry Elzivir," I cried, hugging him. "I am so sorry."

After that, there was little to say. We were
sailing to become slaves on the other side of the
world. All hope was gone of ever seeing Grace,
Moonfleet or freedom again.

The journey was terrible. There was little light
or air below deck and, as the sea grew rougher,
many of the prisoners became badly seasick. A
week passed, and the weather grew worse. The
ship rolled violently over the waves, tossing
us about. Then, one night, the hatch above us
opened and a guard peered down. His face was
white with fear.

"Abandon ship,"
he cried. "We're
sinking!"

Chapter 8
Shipwreck

Elzivir and I scrambled up to the deck. All
around us, waves rose up like mountains. The
guards had gone – and taken all the lifeboats
with them.

"They've left us to die like rats," Elzivir spat. But now I saw something else. There, in the distance, was a line of cliffs.

"Elzivir," I shouted, "those cliffs… We're in Moonfleet Bay!"

Elzivir spotted the cliffs too and a brief smile
flashed across his face. Battling against the
crashing waves, he climbed up to the ship's
steering wheel. "We're not safe yet," he cried,
"I'll try to turn us inland."

There were rocks everywhere and the storm
was getting worse. The other prisoners were
wild with fear. But, gradually, the ship began
to turn.

"John," Elzivir shouted, "look!" He pointed
to a small light, flickering on the cliff top. My
heart soared. Grace said she would
burn a candle until I returned.
Had she waited all this time?

We drew closer and closer to the shore. But then I heard a deafening crash.

"We've hit the rocks," Elzivir shouted. The ship flipped on its side, throwing us all headlong into the sea. Waves hammered down on us. I could see villagers calling from the beach, desperate to help. We had little chance of swimming that far, but we had to try.

We swam for our lives. I saw the villagers throwing a rope for us to catch, then Elzivir grabbing it. He reached out for me, but I heard a thunder from behind and another great wave smashed me to the shallow seabed.

I thought I was going to die, but then someone dragged me back to the surface.

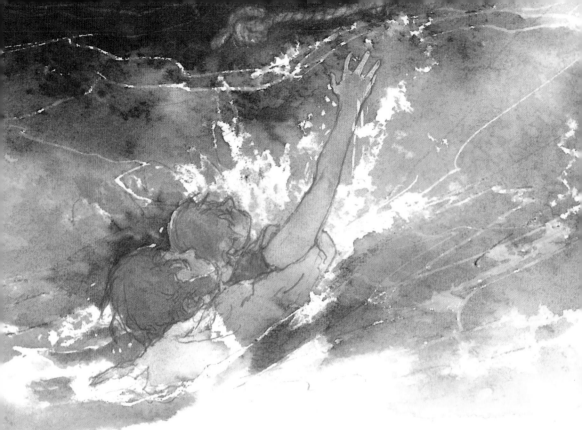

It was Elzivir. He had let go of the rope and swum back to save me. Elzivir pulled me through the waves, swimming for the shore. "The rope," he shouted, "grab the rope, John!"

The villagers' rope was an arm's length away. Just as another wave came, Elzivir shoved me forward with all his might. There was a roar of water and I caught the rope. I felt the line pull, and in seconds I was lying safe on the beach.

I looked for Elzivir, but the wave had dragged him back out to sea. I tried to call his name, but I was numb with cold.

Tears poured down my cheeks as I stared out at the crashing waves. Elzivir had drowned. He had given up his life, here on Moonfleet beach, for me.

Chapter 9
The letter

Morning was breaking as I walked up through
Moonfleet village. The storm had died and
clouds had given way to a brilliant blue sky. The
village looked the same as it had years ago.

There was my aunt's house, the church, and
the *Why Not* inn. I entered the old tavern, and
found it cobwebbed and empty. I lit a fire,
then sat with my head in my hands, crying
for Elzivir.

506

After a while, I felt a light touch on my shoulder. "John," a voice said, "I kept a candle burning for you. But have you forgotten me?"

It was Grace, grown up and more beautiful than ever. She sat with me, and I told her everything that had happened since I last left Moonfleet. "Grace," I said, "I am a broken wretch, with no money."

Grace just smiled and took my hand. "John," she replied, "it is not money that makes a man. Elzivir was right. That treasure was cursed. And if you ever find it again, you must use it to help others."

I was about to ask her what she meant, when
Ratsey came in with Mr. Glennie, the minister.
Both had grown old, but I recognized them
immediately. I told Ratsey how Elzivir had died,
and saw tears in his eyes. Then Mr. Glennie
unfolded an old letter.

"John, do you know someone named Mr.
Aldobrand?" he asked.

"Only too well," I replied, startled. I told them
about the old diamond dealer, and how he had
lied to send Elzivir and me to slavery.

"Well," Mr. Glennie said, "this letter is from
him. It arrived here eight years ago. After you
last saw him, his business collapsed. His
health failed too, and he told people you
had put a curse on him in court."

I remembered my words in the courthouse. *Now you have the treasure, and may it curse you the way it has me.*

"But what have his fortunes to do with me?" I asked.

"Before he died," Mr. Glennie continued, "Mr. Aldobrand lost all of his wealth except the money your diamond brought him. He left that money for you, hoping it would free him from the curse."

And so all of that great fortune became mine. But I never kept a penny for myself. Instead, we gave some to old sailors who needed it the most, and the rest was used to build a new lighthouse above Moonfleet Bay.

I married Grace, and we spent
our days walking in the woods, as we
had years ago. I am older now, and happy.
But I will never forget Elzivir. On stormy nights,
I sit and watch the waves crash over Moonfleet
Bay and remember the night that my friend
saved me.

511

Cover illustration: Kelly Murphy

Edited by Lesley Sims
Designed by Louise Flutter and Sam Chandler
Digital manipulation by Nick Wakeford

First published in 2011 by Usborne Publishing Ltd, 83-85 Saffron Hill,
London EC1N 8RT, England.
www.usborne.com Copyright © 2011 Usborne Publishing Ltd.
 First published in America in 2015. UE.